I SEE THE MOON

BOOKS BY C. B. CHRISTIANSEN

C. B. Christiansen

I SEE

THE MOON

Aladdin Paperbacks

First Aladdin Paperbacks edition April 1996

Aladdin Paperbacks
An imprint of Simon & Schuster
Children's Publishing Division
1230 Avenue of the Americas
New York, NY 10020

The Library of Congress has cataloged the hardcover edition as follows:
Christiansen, C. B.
    I see the moon / by C.B. Christiansen.—1st ed.
      p.   cm.
    Summary: Twelve-year-old Bitte learns the answer to the question, "What is love?" when her older sister decides to place her unborn child for adoption.
    ISBN 0-689-31928-2
    [1. Love—Fiction. 2. Pregnancy—Fiction. 3. Adoption—Fiction.
4. Family life—Fiction. 5. Norwegian Americans—Fiction.]
    I. Title.
PZ7.C45285Iam   1994
[Fic]—dc20   94-10856
ISBN 0-689-80441-5 (Aladdin pbk.)

This is for you

–C. B. C.

ACKNOWLEDGMENTS

The author would like to acknowledge the following authors, experts, and baby-sitters for helping make this book possible: Peggy King Anderson; "Papa"; Roger; Barbara Helen Berger; Daniel A. Farr, Attorney at Law; Mary Kay; Kathryn O. Galbraith; Brenda Z. Guiberson; Tobi Hon-Englund; Nancy Luenn; Pat Mauser; the Nordic Heritage Museum; Mary Paananen; Ellen Rebecca Rees, M.A., Scandinavian Studies, University of Washington; Ida Vandermollen, M.A., Adoption Social Worker; and especially Laura Anderson, our beloved Lo-Lo.

CONTENTS

"Stars," Axel said slowly. "We connect them into groups and patterns, but they are still separate. Each star in the constellation has its own name. Did you know that? Each star has its own identity."

Then the stars are like people in a family, I thought.

Mamma

Pappa

Jorgen
(*YUHR-gen*)

Kari
(*KAR-ee*)

Bitte
(*BIT-teh*)

I SEE THE MOON

Chapter One

YOU

I call you Isabella.
We are connected, you and I.
I made you a promise once and I intend to keep it.

Isabella is not your real name, but it was my favorite name the summer I turned twelve. I wished my parents had given me a long beautiful name instead of a short sharp one. Mamma is Norwegian, so we children have names like Jorgen and Kari and Bitte Liten, which means "tiny." I am the youngest. They called me little Bitte, even when I was twelve.

When I asked Mamma to consider changing my name, she said, "Don't you think there have been enough changes?"

It was true. Our family changed that summer, especially Kari. But Mamma, Pappa, Jorgen and I—we changed, too, the summer I turned twelve.

Twelve.

I am twice that now, and still I have not forgotten.

School was over for the year. I was on my way to seventh grade. I had learned the major exports of Brazil and had moved on to a new subject: love.

My friend Claire had been interested in love for months, since the day she officially became a woman. She had stopped playing softball and started dressing frilly. She had stopped reading adventure books and started reading magazines.

I was different from Claire. I liked reading survival stories. I liked wearing jeans. I liked swinging my wooden bat, hitting ears of corn over the barn, and watching the kernels fly like sweat from a galloping horse.

I was not interested in becoming a woman. I *was* interested in love. What was it? How did it happen? Would it ever happen to me?

You see, Isabella, Claire thought she knew all there was to know about love. But for me it was like trying to learn math without a textbook and without a teacher.

Claire said real love was about holding tight and never letting go. She said it had to do with hugging and kissing and other things, too.

Unimaginable things.

The only boy *I* had ever kissed was Robert McCormick, and that was on a dare. Later, I couldn't remember the feel of his lips at all. I remembered only his nose. It is amazing how big a nostril can look, up close. Amazing and not very romantic.

Claire had groaned when I told her about my first kiss. "Silly," she said, "you should have closed your eyes."

How was I supposed to know, Isabella? Without a textbook. Without a teacher.

I had tried to ask my sister, Kari, about love. After all, she was fifteen and had a boyfriend, shy Angus. Kari and Angus. I was sure they knew about hugging and kissing and holding on forever. But Kari refused to answer my questions about love. "Don't ask me that!" she'd shout. Mamma would hear her and come running. "Leave Kari alone, Bitte. Stop with all your questions."

Mamma was busy that summer, growing vegetables and feeding farmhands while Pappa worked the wheat fields. Her face was tanned as usual. But the sad lines around her eyes were new. The sad lines had come with the changes.

Mamma's arms were full of rhubarb the morning I asked her about love. She had been up early, cutting the red stalks before the sun wilted them. Have you

3

tasted rhubarb, Isabella? It looks like celery without the ridges, and it is more sour than lemons. If you're lucky, you'll have someone like Mamma around who can take a sour rhubarb stalk and make something sweet and delicious of it.

Mamma came into the kitchen hugging her armful of rhubarb. She caught me standing at the counter, reading one of Claire's romance magazines. "*God morgen,* Mamma," I told her. Mamma liked speaking Norwegian, especially with her older brother, Axel. She usually smiled when I tried a Norwegian phrase. That morning she shook her head. "Bitte, Bitte. Are you still reading that *sludder,* that nonsense?"

I cleared my throat. "Well, yes, Mamma. How else am I supposed to learn about love?"

"You don't learn love through magazines." Mamma dumped the rhubarb into the sink and looked out the window to the wheat fields. Then she gave me her tender-Mamma look. "Don't rush it, Bitte. Please."

I guess Mamma didn't remember how it was to be twelve, Isabella. Maybe that was why she had been giving me errands since school let out. Making work for me. Making play. But going to the grocery hadn't helped. Digging potatoes hadn't helped. Cards and checkers and dominoes with my sister, Kari, had not helped answer my question.

"What is love, Mamma? Is it like what Kari and Angus have?"

Mamma lowered her head and murmured something to herself.

I waited for an answer.

"Be useful, now, and wash this rhubarb," Mamma said finally.

I knew better than to ask again. I turned on the faucet, letting the water splash over the rhubarb, letting my thoughts wander to hot pie with ice cream melting down the sides.

Mamma went to work on the crust, mixing flour and shortening with quick fingers. Pappa always said Mamma was a whirlwind in the kitchen, especially in summer when the wheat was ripe and ready for harvest. But I could see it was more than feeding a harvest crew that kept Mamma's hands moving. She had other things on her mind. More important things. Things that had been making her sigh and shake her head and phone her older brother, Axel, for long Norwegian conversations none of us could understand.

I was afraid Mamma didn't have room in her mind for my question. I was wrong.

"Bitte," she said suddenly. "About love . . ."

"Yes?" *Yes?*

Mamma touched my cheek. "You'll know it when you see it." She smiled a sweet smile. But I frowned, feeling sour as the rhubarb. What kind of answer was that? *You'll know it when you see it.* Was that an answer, Isabella? I didn't think so.

Chut! Chut! Chut! I hacked at the rhubarb while Mamma calmly rolled her crust. By the time Jorgen and Pappa came in for breakfast, five pies bubbled in the oven.

My brother and father had already been out in the fields. At seventeen, Jorgen was old enough to have a real job, so Pappa had made him a foreman. Jorgen was going to agricultural college in a year. Whenever I asked him about love, he looked confused. Jorgen seemed to love only the wheat. "It speaks to me," he said, so many times I had started to believe him.

Since Mamma was busy whisking eggs, I poured myself a half cup of coffee and sat down with Jorgen and Pappa. Had Mamma seen? I hoped not. Mamma thought I was too young for coffee, Isabella. Mamma thought I was too young for everything.

Jorgen trickled cream into my cup.

I asked, "What did the wheat say today?"

He leaned forward. "Wouldn't you know it, little Bitte? Today it said, 'Psst. Come to me, Jorgen. Cut me down and plant me again.'"

I nodded. Though wheat had never spoken to me, it seemed like something wheat would say, especially at harvest time.

Mamma moved to the table to set a platter of eggs and ham in front of Pappa. He thanked her with a squeeze. I thought of what Claire once told me: "True love equals Passion with a capital *P*." In that case, Isabella, Mamma and Pappa did not have true love. Love, to them, seemed to have more to do with food than Passion.

When Mamma turned her back, Pappa lifted the lid off the sugar bowl. He scooped out a spoonful and held it over my coffee. He tipped it slowly, letting the sugar drift down like a sweet snowfall.

When the spoon was empty, I looked at Pappa's face. It had gone tight with the changes. His jaw was often clenched, his forehead creased in deep furrows. But he still had his crinkles, Isabella. He still had those gentle wrinkles around his eyes. He smiled at me. I smiled back. Every pappa should have crinkles.

"And you, Pappa," I asked. "Did the wheat talk to you?"

"Of course," he said. "To me it says the same thing every day. It says, 'I will make you a rich man.'"

Jorgen and I laughed at that, Isabella, because farming had not made Pappa rich. It had made him happy. That was why Jorgen wanted to be a farmer, too, and not a businessman in a suit like Mamma's brother, Axel.

"Rich!" Mamma joined in the laughter, the sad lines

leaving her face for a moment. And Pappa joined in, his jaw suddenly open and relaxed. Mamma, Pappa, Jorgen, and I laughed and laughed. Right then, in our farmhouse kitchen, everything seemed normal.

Then we heard my sister's heavy footsteps. Those days, Kari slept in late.

I saw the faces change again. Pappa's tightened. Mamma's sagged. But they smiled at Kari and their smiles were real, Isabella.

"I heard laughing," Kari said in a groggy voice. "What's the joke?"

"Rich farmers," Jorgen answered.

"Oh." Kari chuckled politely. It was an old joke and, besides, the rest of us weren't laughing anymore.

We watched Kari move slowly across the kitchen in her faded pink bathrobe. She looked sleepy faced and puffy eyed. But pretty. Kari was still the prettiest girl in the sophomore class, even with her huge stomach stretching against the tie of her robe. Even with her waddle.

She put her hand to her back and sank into the chair next to mine.

I don't know why we were all so quiet, Isabella. Our silence seemed to follow Kari that summer. The silence made me squirm. "Kari," I blurted, "does wheat talk to you?"

She squinted at me, as if it were too early in the

morning for my games. "No," she said softly, "but I like the sound of it. I guess you'd say it sings to me." Her pretty face woke up a little. "It makes me want to dance."

I pictured Kari waltzing through the wheat fields with shy Angus. I'll be honest, Isabella. I couldn't picture the other thing they had done. The thing that had caused the sad lines in Mamma's face and the miracle that was you, growing inside my sister.

Chapter Two

SECRETS

As the rest of my family ate their breakfast, I stirred my coffee and smiled to myself. Soon I would become your aunt, Isabella. I planned to be just like my Aunt Minna, Axel's wife. Minna and Axel were old, fifteen years older than Mamma and Pappa. Yet Minna had always seemed young. And she was my favorite aunt.

Auntie Minna. Auntie Me. The words sang in my head. I took a big bite of ham and scrambled eggs.

"Slow down, Bitte," Mamma said. "And Kari, drink your juice. It's good for you. Good for you *and* the baby. You both need your strength."

Mamma had been hovering over Kari for months, rubbing her feet at night, rubbing her back in the morning, urging her to eat, sleep, exercise. I could see the hovering bothered Kari sometimes, but she tried not to let it show.

"Kari," Mamma said. "You look pale. Are you feeling all right?"

Kari shrugged, and shifted in her chair. "I feel all right, but I'll be glad when this little one comes."

I took another, smaller bite of food. I'd be glad, too, Isabella. I couldn't wait to become your aunt. *Auntie Bitte. Auntie Me.*

I peeked at Kari's stomach pressed against the breakfast table and thought of the night she told Mamma and Pappa about you. I was upstairs in my room, listening through the heater vent. Their hot words burned in my ears.

"Is Angus the one?" Pappa had asked. "Is Angus the father?"

Kari must have nodded, because Pappa was silent then. A scary silence. A roar without a noise.

I thought I heard Mamma crying, something I hadn't heard very often. "So young," she said. "So young." Mamma had been nearly twice Kari's age when she'd had her own babies. And Mamma's mamma had been older still, at Mamma's birth. "I came fifteen years after my brother," Mamma had told me once. "I was an unexpected blessing." You were an unexpected blessing, too, Isabella. That was my very first thought. But Mamma's first thought was about Kari. "What about your future?" Mamma asked.

I didn't hear an answer. Maybe Kari didn't have an

answer. But I did. A small farm town like ours could be cruel to an unmarried girl expecting a baby, Isabella. I knew that. But the real world had never troubled Kari before. Her life had always seemed like a fairy tale to me. She was pretty. She was happy. She was able to do anything she set her mind to doing. She had many friends, including Angus. With Angus she had Passion. And now she was going to have a sweet baby girl. Actually, no one knew for sure you were a girl. But I hoped it with all my heart. Soon Kari was going to have you, Isabella. So why couldn't her fairy tale continue? Why were the voices floating up through the heater vent so filled with worry?

The next morning, when Mamma told me her version of the news, she tried to keep the worry from her cool, hushed voice. But it had been there. Invisible, but not invisible. Like heat waves rising.

After that, the secrets began. As the months went by, I overheard muffled conversations lasting late into the night. Long talks between Kari and Mamma. Long talks between Pappa and Mamma. And silences, louder than words, between Jorgen and Pappa.

Secrets were shared, but not with me.

"Ask them!" Claire had nagged. "Why not find out what's going on?"

In Claire's family, she asked questions and got answers. In my family, I asked questions and got nowhere. *You're too young to understand. We'll tell you when the time is right. You'll find out soon enough.*

When I told Claire I was getting worried about the secrets, she said, "Don't worry. Things will work out for Kari and Angus, just like in the magazine stories." A life of sweetness and light was how Claire had described it.

Sweetness and light, I thought, as I stared at my coffee, lightened and sweetened with sugar and cream. I wanted to taste it, but Mamma was hovering again. "Don't grow up so fast," she kept saying to me, those days and months while you got bigger and stronger inside Kari. "What's your hurry, Bitte Liten?"

I wasn't little Bitte anymore. I had my dreams of love. I had my sorry excuse of a first kiss. I had my memories of Robert McCormick's nostrils. It made me sigh just to think of them—those big nostrils, round and dark with tiny hairs inside. I sighed again to think what a disappointment Passion with a capital *P* had been.

"Something wrong, Bitte?" Mamma asked.

I shook my head. Mamma wouldn't like hearing about my kiss, Isabella, sorry or not. "No, nothing's wrong," I said.

"That's good." Mamma gave my shoulder a friendly pat. Then she lifted my coffee cup before I'd tasted even one sip. Like nearly every other morning on the farm, she dumped the creamy sweetness down the drain and replaced it with a glass of pure milk.

I sighed even louder than before. I didn't want to become a woman, like Claire, but I was tired of being too young for this and too young for that. I was tired of being left out.

I sipped my milk and thought of Minna. She would have let me drink coffee with cream. She would have told me about love and about Kari and about the future. Minna had always included me in everything. No wonder she was my favorite aunt. Minna would have let me in on the secrets.

That's what favorite aunts are for, I realized. I made a vow right then, Isabella, a solemn promise to let you in on secrets, if I ever knew any.

You must have jumped for joy at my promise because Kari gasped—"oh!"—and leaned back in her chair.

"Is it time?" I asked. "Is it time for the baby?"

Kari pushed her breath out slowly. She shook her head. "No, not for another month, according to the doctor."

"And then it will be over," Mamma soothed.

Over? What a strange thing to say, I thought. Because, really, it would just be starting. Kari's new life. Her fairy-tale future.

She would be a junior in the fall. A junior in high

school with a baby and a husband. I hadn't seen shy Angus for a while, but I sensed he was staying clear of Pappa's clenched jaw and Jorgen's clenched fists.

I was certain things would be different once Kari and Angus were married.

Claire and I talked about it a few days later while we drank pink lemonade on our front porch. Planning a future for you and Kari and Angus was one of our favorite pastimes, Isabella.

"Find out when in heaven's name they're getting married," Claire demanded. "Maybe we can be in the wedding." Claire sat cross-legged on the porch, turning the pages of a bridal magazine she had bought that morning. She stopped at a picture of bridesmaids. "I look gorgeous in mauve," she said.

I leaned closer to see what "mauve" was. A big sticky drop of my lemonade plopped onto the slick page.

Claire frowned.

"I think Kari and Angus will get married after the baby's born," I told her.

Claire raised her eyebrows.

I knew what she was thinking: it wasn't the usual way things were done, especially in our small town.

"No one will care," I said firmly.

"Of course not," Claire dabbed at the wet spot on the page of bridesmaids. "They'll marry and move to their dream house," she said eagerly.

We loved talking about your dream house, Isabella. We had already decided it would be a small house because Angus didn't make much money as a box boy and he didn't get paid at all for the work he did on his family's farm. It would be a small, wonderful house.

"The house still has the white picket fence, right?" Claire said.

"Yes," I answered, "and the arched trellis covered with roses, like on the cover of that book we saw."

"Red roses or pink?" Claire asked, as she always did.

"Maybe both," I said, as I always did. "It will have an arched trellis, painted white to match the fence, and"—we always added something new, Isabella—"and . . . the smell of raisin cookies coming from the kitchen."

"And . . . ," Claire said, "you and I will baby-sit so Kari and Angus can walk, no, *stroll* beneath the trellis holding hands."

I finished my lemonade. "They'll be poor, but happy. Don't you think?"

"Mmm-hmm." Claire closed her eyes. "It's so romantic. Romantic with a capital *R*. I'm glad it's not *my* sister, though."

I jumped to my feet. I needed to move, Isabella. Do you ever need to move your body away from your thoughts? I stretched my arms and legs. "Come on, Claire, don't you want to play ball or something?"

Claire wrinkled her nose. "No, thanks. I've got things to do." She picked up her bridal magazine and went home to paint her nails or curl her hair or one of those other "official woman" things.

I headed for the backyard. Mamma was kneeling in the garden, weeding, while Kari sat on the grass with her face to the sun. My shadow fell across them. Kari looked up at me with a sad smile. I wanted to change it to a glad smile.

Wedding talk was happy talk, I always thought. The brides in Claire's magazine looked happy. Their mothers looked happy. Their fathers, sisters, and brothers all hugged each other and grinned in the magazine. So I asked, "Kari, when you and Angus get married, will it be a big wedding or a small one?"

Kari's eyes got round. "Wedding?" she whispered. She did not look like a happy bride.

"Yes, wedding," I said. "You know, W-E-D-D—"

"Oh, Bitte, I heard you the first time." She drew tiny hearts in the dirt. "I'm not ready, though. Not ready for that. Not yet."

"Well, when?"

Kari brushed the dirt lightly, erasing the hearts. She wouldn't look at me. "Well, never. Not to Angus. It would never last."

"Never last?" This didn't sound like the Kari I knew. I glanced at Mamma. Was she as shocked as I? No,

Isabella, she did not seem surprised by Kari's words.

Finally, Kari looked at me. "I can't marry Angus, Bitte. I just . . . I don't even want to. I'm too young. Way too young."

Too young? I thought I was the too-young one. I tried to understand, but Kari's words would not sink in. They didn't fit with my fairy-tale plans. And what would Claire say?

I felt the breath go out of me.

No wedding.

That was the first secret.

Chapter Three

AND MORE
SECRETS

I watched Kari sifting the soil in Mamma's garden. She was sure about her decision to not marry Angus. I could see that. When she told me she was too young to be a bride, she really believed it. Marrying Angus was not something Mamma had taken away from her, like a cup of creamy sweet coffee.

No, Isabella, it was not like that at all.

"I suppose some people can manage being married at fifteen," Kari said, "but I'm not one of them. I know it in my heart, Bitte." Her eyes followed the movement of a bee buzzing in and out of Mamma's squash blossoms.

Even though the sun felt warm, my skin prickled with goose bumps. There was another secret, Isabella. I could almost smell it in the garden air. I started for the back door. I didn't think I was ready for a second secret.

"Where are you going?" Mamma called.

"I have things to do," I shouted over my shoulder.

"Bitte!" Kari rose heavily to her feet. "Wait!" But the screen door slammed on her words.

I climbed the stairs to my room, wondering again what Claire would say about this latest piece of news: no wedding. She would probably say that the life Kari had chosen would be even more Romantic because it would be even more of a struggle.

Kari already knew about struggle, Isabella.

She had finished her sophomore year of high school growing seven months of baby under her school clothes. There were whispers. There were jokes. You will learn, Isabella, that this is the way of some people.

Kari had tried to ignore them. She had taken good care of herself for your sake. She had studied hard for her own sake. Mamma and Pappa and Jorgen and I had all been proud of her.

When Claire and I opened our report cards, we found only average grades. "But Kari got straight As," I bragged.

"Ha!" Claire said, "I'll bet she got an A-plus in sex education!"

I squeezed a bruise into Claire's arm that day. It turned an ugly purple and lasted for a week. I was glad. After all, I hadn't expected my best friend to tease me about my sister.

I had learned to expect it from other people, though. They said, "Bitte, I hear your sister is going to have a baby." And their eyes would get big, and they would talk to me from behind their hands. "Is it true? Your sister is going to be a *mother?*" I shrugged them off. Whose business was it anyway? Not theirs. But I was a little disappointed no one said, "Bitte, I hear you're going to be an *aunt.* Is it true?" I would have said, "Yes. Oh, yes! It's true!"

From the moment news of you rose through the heater vent to warm my imagination, I had been making plans for us. We had so much to look forward to, Isabella. I would be your aunt and you would be my little niece and we would love each other. Just like Minna and me.

Minna. My favorite aunt. By the time I was twelve, she had filled a photograph album with pictures of the two of us: Minna holding a tiny, squinting Bitte up to the sunlight; a bigger Bitte sitting on Minna's kitchen counter waving a wooden spoon over a bowl of raisin-cookie dough; our two silhouettes at the edge of a pond—one large, one small—telling stories and toasting marshmallows under the night sky. Those photographs and more had been carefully pasted into Minna's album.

When I got to my bedroom, I saw our latest picture framed on my dresser. Axel had sent it, along with a letter, a few months earlier. I picked it up and studied it. The two of us stood beside her rosebushes, Minna staring at the camera with a terrible question in her eyes. But what question? I wondered. Ever since her last birthday, Minna had been forgetting things like who, what, where, when, why. "This sometimes happens at our age," Axel had written. Minna had moved from their house by the pond soon after the picture was taken. "To a home for people who forget," Axel had written. I hadn't seen her since. Not since the blooming of her winter roses. "Remember the happy times," Axel had written.

I set the photograph back on my dresser. I didn't need pictures to remind me of our good times together. Laughing, loving, wondering.

I was eager to do those things with you, Isabella.

Auntie Me. Auntie Me. Maybe Kari was not going to be the wife of shy Angus. Maybe they were not going to have a fairy-tale future. Maybe the three of you were not going to live in a little house with a rose-covered trellis and the smell of raisin cookies coming from the kitchen.

"But I'll still be Auntie Me." I said the words out loud.

"Did you say something?" Kari stood at my door holding a flat white box.

I shook my head.

"May I come in?" Kari asked.

I nodded reluctantly. We sat on my bed with the box between us.

"So," I said, "you're going to be a single mother."

Kari looked puzzled. She probably wondered how I knew about such things. I had read about single motherhood in Claire's magazines.

"What will you do?" I asked. "Will you live at home?" A little bubble of excitement grew in my chest. *You and me, together, Isabella. Together in the kitchen. Together in the wheat fields. More together, even, than Minna and I had been.*

Kari nodded. "I'll still live at home, but . . ."

"Don't worry about space," I said. "I'll share my room. I'll be glad to share my room with the baby."

"That's a really nice offer," Kari said. She rubbed her hand over her stomach, over you. "This baby deserves the best."

"The very, very best," I said, planning how I'd move my bed so your crib could stand by the window and catch the morning light. Kari's idea of not getting married began to seem like a good one. Without Angus, without a husband, Kari would need my help.

I would get to spend even more time with you, Isabella.

"Bitte, I told you I'm too young to get married"— Kari looked at me with her soft blue eyes—"and I'm too young to be a single mother." Kari patted you again through her maternity clothes. "I don't think I would do a good enough job. It's an important job."

"You're just tired now, Kari," I soothed, trying to sound like Mamma. "After the baby's born, I'll help you. You can do it, Kari. You can." Couldn't Kari do anything she set her mind to doing?

Kari shook her head. "No, Bitte. I can't. Listen to me, though." She touched my arm. "I've found a really good home for my baby."

Home for my baby. *Home for my baby?* I shivered, suddenly feeling ice cold from the inside out. In all my planning, Isabella, it had never occurred to me that Kari might be making different plans.

Or had it?

Had it? I was shocked, Isabella, yet hadn't my suspicions been gathering all along? Hadn't I brushed them away the way Kari had brushed away her drawings in the dirt? I shivered once more. My raisin-cookie, arched-trellis dream house filled my mind and then began to fade. "Home?" I asked weakly.

"Yes, a home," Kari said. "A nice house. Two—"

"Wait," I interrupted. "I get it. Of course you've found a good home. *Our* house."

Kari shook her head.

Not our house.

"Why didn't you tell me?" I asked finally. Why hadn't Kari warned me before I'd dreamed a life for us, Isabella? Wasn't I part of the family? Wasn't I the aunt?

Kari sighed. "To be honest, Mamma thought you were too young to understand."

I pressed my lips together at that because Mamma had been half right. I didn't understand. I stared at my sister and tried to read what was in her mind and heart. "You say you want the best for your baby, but it sounds like you're thinking of sending her away. It sounds like you're thinking of sending her to live with *strangers.*"

Kari's face turned bright red, as if I had slapped one cheek and then the other. But she didn't blink. She stared right back at me and said, "Every parent is a stranger at first. Every parent and child have to get to know each other in the beginning. Besides, these are not strangers the way you mean. I chose them."

"You chose?" I asked. That wasn't the way it worked, Isabella. Not in those days. Not in our town. "When did you choose?" I demanded. "How did you choose?"

"I thought about the kind of life I want for my baby, her *or* him," Kari said. "We found a lawyer. Finally. It took forever to find a lawyer who would help me do it my way, so I could be a part of what was happening. He really listened to me, and then he showed me pictures of families." Kari opened the flat white box and pulled out a photograph album. She turned to the first page and pointed to a couple, not as young as Kari and Angus, not as old as Mamma and Pappa. "This is the couple I chose," she said quietly. "Their album tells a lot about them. And last week, Mamma and Pappa and I met them in person."

"You met them?" I felt my eyes widen.

"I had to," Kari said. "I had to see them for myself."

I could hardly believe my ears, Isabella. All this had gone on behind my back. Claire had been wrong. I had been right to worry about the secrets.

"Look," Kari said, turning the pages. "This is their house. And see here? Two cats, one in each lap."

I saw pictures, Isabella. That was all. Those people were not real. Their cats were not real. I squeezed my eyes shut. I thought of the album I'd planned for you and me, filled with memories of the things we were going to do together. At first, quiet tears leaked from my closed eyes, but my crying got louder until Kari noticed, and I found myself sobbing in her arms.

I pulled back. "No one told me," I accused again. "Why?"

Kari folded the album shut. "We wanted to wait until it was settled."

Settled, Isabella. Kari's future and yours. And mine, too, because there would be no Auntie Me.

Kari put the album on my pillow. "I had dreams, Bitte, about Angus and the baby and being all together. But they were just dreams. I had to stop dreaming and make real plans for my baby."

Dreams? Plans? What about *my* dreams and plans? Had anyone thought about me? No, they had not. I couldn't listen anymore. I pressed my hands over my ears. I even hummed, Isabella. Wasn't that childish? Well, I didn't care.

I turned away from Kari. I turned toward the bedroom window where your crib might have stood. The fields were blanketed with wheat. I thought I could hear the wheat heads rustle, *shh, shh, shh,* the way they do in a soft breeze. I thought maybe the wheat was going to speak to me as it spoke to my brother, Jorgen. I took my hands from my ears.

"*Shh.*" It was not the wheat talking. It was Mamma, standing in the doorway to my room. "Hush, now. Stop humming and listen."

"It hasn't been easy," Kari said. "I had to think of

29

what was best for this little person. And the best choice seems to be—"

I knew what was coming, Isabella, and I didn't want to hear it. "Don't say it," I begged. "Don't say the word."

Kari leaned closer. "It's not a bad word, Bitte." And gently, gently she whispered it.

Chapter Four

IF ONLY

I stared at the full-length mirror on my bedroom wall. It reflected Mamma and Kari, and me standing apart from them. Kari had just told me of her plans for you. *If only,* I thought. If only Kari and Angus were older. If only Kari had told me earlier. If only she hadn't whispered the word and made it all real.

Adoption.

If only Minna could be here, I thought. She would know what to do. If only Minna hadn't gone away.

*If only*s don't make things better, Isabella. *If only* is what you say when there's no hope left. But hopeless was how I felt. Hopeless and helpless.

"If you really loved your baby, you wouldn't do this," I said.

"Bitte!" Mamma scolded.

"It's okay, Mamma." Kari looked at me with the

most serious eyes I have ever seen. "You're wrong, Bitte. I do love this baby."

I blinked. Love? This was not the kind of love they talked about in Claire's magazines. What about holding on tight? What about never letting go? I wanted to ask, but Kari stared me down with her serious eyes.

Later that night, those same questions kept bothering me. I found Kari in her room, at the sewing machine. I sat beside her and watched her prepare to stitch the final seam on your baby quilt. I was part of that quilt, Isabella. I had added a piece from my own baby quilt to all the other patches we had collected. Then Kari and Mamma had arranged the patches. What was once a jumble of colors and shapes now fit together to form a pattern, with each piece in its own perfect place.

I had thought the quilt would lie in the crib beneath my bedroom window. Now I didn't know what to think. "It's beautiful, Kari," I said. "But what will you do with it?"

Kari smiled to herself. "I'll send it with the baby. I want the baby to have something special from me. From us."

I cleared my throat. "I just wish . . ."

"So do I," Kari said, reading my mind. She hugged the quilt to herself. Then she lined up the edges and guided them carefully through the sewing machine.

Minna had taught us both to sew, and Kari was very good at it. Still, I stared at my sister. How could she be so calm? Didn't she care? The sewing machine hummed along. Suddenly the rattle of a loose bobbin filled the room.

Kari groaned. She raised the needle and pulled the quilt from the machine. "Oh, look what I've done!"

A tangled thread looped its way along the seam she had sewn.

"It's not so bad," I lied.

"It is, too!" Kari buried her face in the fabric. "I'll never be able to straighten it out!"

I watched my sister cry, Isabella. I don't know how or why, but I knew it was the right thing to do, letting Kari cry into your quilt, letting her spill some of her tears so she wouldn't have so many to carry around. When she finally raised her head, there were wet marks on the patchwork. Her tears had become part of the pattern.

I had come to ask questions, but the timing was all wrong. Instead, I held out my hand. Kari passed me the quilt. I worked the threads loose the way Minna had taught me. When I handed the quilt back, the tangles were gone and Kari's tears had dried.

The stitching went smoothly the next time. Unless someone told you, Isabella, you wouldn't know the effort that went into that seam.

Once it was stitched together, Kari and I held the quilt between us. Under the yellow circle of her bedroom lamplight, we tucked the cotton batting with twenty-four tiny bows.

"Minna would be proud," I said.

Kari nodded. She seemed relaxed now that the sewing was done. "I always loved our trips to Minna and Axel's house."

"Me, too."

Kari giggled. "Remember your make-believe mouse family?"

"Minna called it the mythical mouse family: Mother mouse, Father mouse, and teeny, tiny . . ." I stopped.

"Baby mouse," Kari finished. We were both quiet.

"You can still change your mind," I blurted. "Can't you, Kari? I mean, if only . . ." If only *what*, I wasn't sure.

Kari found the patch that had come from her own baby quilt. She rubbed it gently. "I've talked to so many people about this. So many people."

"I didn't know," I said. She hadn't talked to me.

"I listened to them all, Bitte. I even fought with some of them because I had to do what felt best to me. I just couldn't stand not knowing where my baby was going." Kari's face darkened into a stubborn scowl. Then it brightened. "Have you looked at the album again? Don't you think I've chosen the right parents?"

I shook my head. "You and Angus are the right parents."

"It takes more than making a baby to be a good parent."

I rolled my eyes. There Kari went, sounding like a grown-up, sounding like all those people she had talked to instead of me. "You know what I think?" I said. "I think you could do it if you really wanted to."

Kari spoke softly. "You know what I think, little Bitte? I think you still live in a make-believe world."

I stood up, letting the quilt drop to the floor. We had been having such a nice time, Isabella. Why did Kari have to go and spoil everything? "I'd rather live in my world than yours," I shouted. I ran from Kari's room, bumping into Mamma on the way out.

I didn't tell Mamma I was sorry, Isabella. I was sure she had been listening outside the door. Yes, I had almost knocked her down, but didn't it serve her right for eavesdropping?

I had a hard time sleeping that night, thinking about my family and how they had kept their secrets from me. I cried into my pillow, then threw it across the room. I wasn't going to give up on your fairy-tale future, Isabella.

The next day, I wrote out a schedule of baby-sitting: when school started, I would come home on my lunch break, and I would also take over for Kari after classes so she could study. I thought I was giving her serious proof I could help, but when I showed Kari my schedule, she laughed. *Laughed.*

Mamma did not laugh when she heard about it. She gripped my shoulders. "Kari has made her decision," she said. "It was a hard decision, hard on all of us. She needs assurance now, that she's done the right thing. So no more discussions, Bitte. I'm warning you. Enough."

It wasn't enough. Not for me. A few days later, while I was shopping with Claire, we saw a tiny T-shirt in the window of a maternity shop. The words *I Love Mommy* were written across the front.

"If this doesn't do it, nothing will," Claire said. She prodded me into the shop.

I bought the shirt and left it on Kari's bed. It was so little and cute, it would surely change her mind. But Kari never saw the shirt. Mamma found it first. She brought it to my room with news: I was going away. "To Axel and Minna's house at the pond," Mamma said. "I know you like it there."

"But Minna's not there anymore. Why do I have to go now?" I asked, even though I knew why, Isabella.

Mamma held up the little shirt. "Your sister has not had an easy time of it. Can you imagine how this would have made her feel?"

I tried to look innocent. "I just thought . . ."

"No, you *didn't* think." Mamma started pulling clothes from my closet. "I'll help you pack," she said firmly. "Axel will come for you tomorrow morning."

"How long do I have to stay?"

Mamma's voice softened. "Just until the baby's born. Just until the baby's home with his or her new parents."

"But that could be a month!"

"I have to think of Kari," Mamma said.

"That's all anyone ever thinks of anymore."

Mamma stopped packing and cupped my face between her hands. "Remember I love you, too, Bitte. We all love you."

"It'll be lonely without Minna," I said. "I hardly know Axel." Though Mamma's family had moved to this country when Axel was twenty, he sometimes acted as if he'd just come from Norway. "It's been forty years," I complained. "Why does he always have to tell those old Norwegian stories?"

"I've told you how we lost our own parents, Pappa then Mamma, right before Jorgen was born?" Mamma tilted her head. "I think the stories are Axel's way of keeping them alive."

"Well, I hope he'll speak English," I said.

Mamma smiled. "Give Axel a chance. He'll be lonely, too."

Late the next morning, I sat on the front porch with my suitcase. I waited for the sound of my uncle's new car, the big 1978 sedan he'd bought when he retired. He and Minna had called it their traveling car. But the longest trip they'd taken was to Minna's new home. I sighed. Did anyone's dreams ever come true? I turned around at the squeak of the screen door.

Kari waddled across the porch and sat beside me. "Maybe someday you'll understand," she said.

I didn't answer. I knew I'd never understand.

"Will you at least take this with you?" Kari tried to hand me her photo album.

I set it aside. Minna's album would be at the pond, but not Minna. "It'll be just me and Axel," I said, "all by ourselves." I wanted to make Kari feel guilty. The thought of staying with my favorite aunt would have given me something to look forward to, Isabella. But with Minna gone and you going, I had nothing to look forward to. Nothing.

It was all Kari's fault. Kari and the rest of my family. That is why, when Axel came, I got into his big new car and didn't say good-bye—not to Mamma or Pappa or Jorgen, either. I left Kari's album behind. And when Axel had said his hellos to the family and climbed back in the car and started the motor, I crossed my arms over my chest and squeezed them tight. Kari waved to me from the front porch. I did not wave back.

"You forgot something?" Axel asked.

I glanced at Kari, her hand stuck in midair. "No."

Axel turned off the motor. "*Ja*, Bitte, I think you did."

I got out of the car slowly and walked toward the house, toward my sister, Kari, and her open arms. She looked so young right then, Isabella. Too young to be married. Too young to be a mother. Too young, even, to be an older sister. But whose fault was that? Not mine.

When I reached the porch, Kari pulled me into her arms. "I'm really scared, you know?" Kari's breath ruffled my hair. "Please wish me luck."

"Good luck," I mumbled to Kari, but I meant it for you, Isabella. I stood to one side and patted Kari's stomach. "If only . . ." I shrugged. Axel was waiting. It was too late for *if only*s.

"If only you would look at the album," Kari suggested.

When I picked it up off the porch, the album fell open to the last page, to a photograph of a couple holding hands under a trellis. I gasped. It was a picture right out of your fairy-tale future, Isabella. "Roses," I whispered.

Beneath the roses stood the man and woman Kari had chosen to be your parents. I didn't want to know anything about those people, but the question came anyway. The words tumbled out before I could stop them. "What are their names?"

Kari touched the picture twice. "Jacob," she said, "and Hope."

Chapter Five

SPEAKING OF HOPE

Axel's big new car led us away from home and Kari and you, Isabella.

"Do you want to be the navigator?" Axel asked.

I shook my head. I wasn't in the mood for navigating the four-hour drive to Axel's house. "Did you know about Hope and Jacob, too?"

Axel nodded.

"Hope," I said. "I hoped for a niece. I hoped to be an aunt, like Minna. That's why I tried to change Kari's mind. I wasn't trying to make things harder for her. Mamma won't listen. First she keeps secrets from me and then she sends me away. It's not fair." I clamped my mouth shut before I said more. After all, Isabella, it was Axel who was listening, not Minna. I didn't know how he would respond.

Axel ran his hand through his fine white hair, the

way he did when he was about to tell one of his Norwegian tales. "*Ja,* you have been sent away from home. It brings to my mind the story of Erik the Red, the Viking who was banished from his homeland. But you will go home again, after Kari's baby comes. That is the difference between you and Erik the Red. And there is another difference, too. He was a mean one, that Erik. But you are not mean, Bitte. You would not hurt Kari on purpose. *Nei.* You are kindhearted. That is one of the things Minna always loved about you and Kari—both kindhearted young girls, the daughters she never had."

Axel and Minna had no daughters *or* sons, Isabella. But for thirty-seven years they had each other. When Axel retired, they had joked about growing old and wrinkled together. And then Minna had started to forget so many whos and whys and whats and wheres and whens that Axel had sadly moved her to the home for people who forget.

I wondered if Axel still sat by the pond in the evenings, stargazing and stoking the campfire. I wondered if he felt small, all by himself under that big dark sky.

"Is it lonely without Minna?" I asked.

"Mmm. *Ja.* I miss her."

"Then why not have her move back home?"

"I wish I could." Axel shifted gears. "I tried to take

care of her, but she needed more than I could give her. Ah, it is hard when you want to take care of someone and you are too old, like me. Or too young . . ."

I hesitated. "Like Kari?" I asked.

Axel and I both glanced at the album sitting between us.

I closed my eyes. Too young. Too old. Was anyone ever exactly the right age?

"You're confused," Axel said.

I nodded. "I'm confused."

Arriving at the cabin confused me even more. It was the same place, but a different place, the way Minna had been the same person but a different person the last time I had seen her. Minna's garden was full of color, but the soil beneath was parched, and weeds sprouted where she would never have allowed them. Her roses bloomed red and pink against the house, but the gray paint behind them was cracked and peeling.

The inside of the house seemed different, too, without Minna there to keep it fresh and clean. But the guest room was the same as it had always been.

Axel had been busy. The smell of lemon oil lingered in the air. The curtains were open, letting sunlight in to form a patch of yellow on the floor. I kicked off my shoes and stood on the bright spot. Through the polished windowpanes, I could see the pond. I smiled, thinking of all the sweet sunlit hours Kari and I had spent here. Things had been so much simpler then.

"Make yourself at home," Axel said. "I'll leave you to your unpacking."

After Axel left, I tucked my few belongings into empty drawers and cupboards. Then I opened the nightstand drawer. I laughed out loud, Isabella, at what I found there: a mouse bed. Minna had always kept the nightstand drawer stocked with little rectangular mattresses just big enough for a mouse to sleep on. Kari and I had made up stories about the mythical mouse family who slept on the beds.

There was just one mouse mattress left, with its bedding crumpled beside it. I recognized one of the little fitted sheets Minna had sewn. Once there had been three of them. Three fitted sheets and three knitted blankets and three patchwork quilts we had pieced together from summer clothes Kari and I had outgrown.

I thought of Kari in her faded pink bathrobe. She had outgrown *all* her summer clothes the past few months. As you grew bigger, Isabella, so had Kari. I sadly smoothed the one tiny sheet that was left, and the one blanket and the one quilt. Where had the others gone? I didn't know. I only knew I would never get to play mouse games with you, Isabella. We could have had so much fun. My make-believe mouse family lived in a world where I could cause things to turn out the way I wanted them to turn out. And, as Minna had often said, "No mice ever had finer beds."

Kari and I had been proud of those beds.

Then a strange thing happened, Isabella. One summer, when I got out the mattresses, Kari turned red in the face and snapped, "Don't play with those like that."

Surprised, I dropped the mattresses. "Why not?"

"Just put them away! Those are not playthings." Kari lowered her voice. "Those are about becoming a woman."

"What do you mean?" I asked, but Kari wouldn't tell. That had hurt my feelings more than her snapping, Isabella. Later, Claire told me what our mouse mattresses were really called: sanitary napkins. And she told me what they were really for: absorbing blood. Still, I didn't understand why Kari had gotten so upset. What did it hurt to play with them? Couldn't we pretend?

Minna was a woman, and she hadn't minded. Had she? If only Minna would walk through that guest-room door, I would ask her, I thought. But Minna wasn't going to come through that door. Kari wasn't going to forget her plans for you, Isabella. And I wasn't going to be an aunt. In the real world, I couldn't cause things to turn out the way I wanted them to turn out.

In the real world, I couldn't stop the changes. You might laugh at this, Isabella: I thought about locking myself in the guest room where everything had stayed the same. How long could I last? A week? A month? Not even an hour. By the time Axel called me to dinner, I was hungry already. So I opened the door and walked back out into the real world.

Axel and I didn't talk much during our meal nor while we carried the dishes to the kitchen. We were silent as we walked the path to the pond and began our old routine of gathering wood for the campfire. After Axel quietly stacked the wood, we sat on the smooth-worn stumps we used as seats. When he set a match to the fire, the crackling mixed with the chirping of the crickets. Then, Isabella, our throats opened up and words poured out. Small talk. Big ideas. Old stories. New tales.

This became our habit.

As that first night passed, and then the next, our talk turned more and more to Minna, until on the third night Axel said, "I will visit Minna tomorrow. You will come?"

"Oh yes!" I answered. I tried to imagine Minna without the pond. Would it be as odd-seeming as the pond without Minna? I would find out. "Tomorrow," I murmured.

"*Ja*, tomorrow," Axel said. "You will see Minna, but

it won't be the way it used to be. Do you understand, Bitte? She forgets things. She may not remember . . . everything."

"Then I will remember for both of us," I said. Sitting out under the night sky, it was hard not to remember Minna and her stories and her singing.

"I remember the moon song," I said. "Do you, Axel?"

"Of course." And to prove it, Axel began to sing. I joined him. Our words floated through the trees and across the still water of the pond:

"I see the moon. The moon sees me.
The moon sees the one I long to see.
So God bless the moon. And God bless me.
And God bless the one I long to see."

"Minna used to sing me to sleep with that song," I told Axel. "She called it Bitte's special lullaby. I can almost hear her voice."

Axel nodded. "*Ja,* I know what you mean."

"It's funny," I said. "I think of Minna's voice as sweet, but it was really kind of scratchy and croaky, wasn't it?"

Axel laughed. "*Ja,* and off-key, too."

We both smiled in the firelight. Minna's wonderfully awful singing was sweet, but not in the usual way.

As if our singing had coaxed it out of hiding, the moon rose above the trees. It was a fat crescent of a moon, a waning moon, and I wondered, Did it really see the ones I longed to see? Did it see Minna? Did it see you, Isabella, inside my sister, Kari?

The moon rose higher and the stars grew bright.

Axel threw a stone into the pond. After the splash, he said, "Our ancestors sailed by these same stars, you know. The Vikings." He pronounced it "wikings."

I had heard Axel's "wiking" stories before. I knew the Vikings were brave and adventurous warriors. But Axel didn't speak of battles or enemy ships that night, Isabella. Instead, he spoke of families—of husbands and fathers and lovers who sailed by the stars on voyages to other lands.

"Those Vikings," said Axel, "they had to be rough in order to survive. But they had their tender sides, too. After a voyage, they returned to their homeland with longships filled with gold and silk and spices and jewels. You can imagine how happy and proud they felt to be bringing treasures to their sweethearts from afar."

Treasures to their sweethearts from afar. Claire would adore that phrase, I thought. And why wouldn't she? Sweethearts and treasures sounded like the perfect ingredients for love. Love with a capital *L*.

Love.

Mamma had said I would know it when I saw it. I stared at the fat crescent moon. Mamma was usually right about things.

Was that changing, too?

Chapter Six

JOURNEYS

The next morning, Axel and I made our way toward Minna. When we crossed the bridge at Danfarr, I was reminded of the different kinds of water I loved: I loved the pond; I loved the ocean; I even loved our public swimming pool. Water. Beautiful water. I watched it rush by beneath the bridge, so different from the land, so different from the wheat fields of home.

Axel's big car hit a pothole.

"Oh!" I said, bounced out of my thoughts.

"You were smiling," Axel said. "What were you thinking?"

"I was thinking how much I like water," I answered. "It's hard to put into words, but it makes me feel . . . alive. I don't know why, though."

"You don't?"

I shook my head.

"It's the Viking blood," Axel said.

"Viking blood?"

"*Ja,* from your ancestors. They built the finest boats in the world, the longships. They were challenged by the sea. They were drawn to the water and you are, too."

Our journey to Minna's wasn't much like those long-ago voyages of the Vikings. The breeze brought dust instead of cool salt air. And Axel, with his short white hair and skinny arms looked nothing like the brawny, red-bearded Vikings I had seen pictured in books.

We didn't travel to exotic lands, Isabella. Instead, we cast anchor at the Save-More store just off the freeway. I followed Axel to the produce section, past islands of oranges and mountains of grapes. We came to a stop at the banana bin.

Axel frowned at the selection. "*Nei,*" he mumbled to himself, picking up overripe banana bunches and setting them aside. "*Nei, nei.*"

I followed him out of the store. "I'm not hungry anyway," I said. "Are you?"

Axel didn't answer.

I shrugged to myself. The bananas at the second store didn't look bad to me. As we left, empty-handed, I asked, "How about apples?"

Axel shook his head.

Finally, we stopped at Gunnarsen's Roadside Fruit Stand, where Axel found the perfect bunch. Ripe, but not too ripe. Firm, but not green. Gorgeous golden yellow skins. Axel held them in front of me. "Look," he said, "not one bruise."

I had to agree: they were flawless. But what a lot of effort, Isabella. Forty-five minutes out of our way for a silly bunch of bananas.

Axel set them gently on the scales. The man behind the stand grinned. "Hello, Axel! You found some good ones today, did you?"

"*Ja*, Mr. Gunnarsen." Axel grinned back. "Only the best for my Minna."

I blushed. Oh, I thought. Not for me. For Minna.

We got back on the freeway and took Exit 109, headed west onto Washington Street, turned right at the bank, left at the church, and right again onto Willow Avenue. I guess we Vikings are good at remembering directions, Isabella.

"Here we are," Axel said.

The small brick building where Minna lived had lots of windows to let the sunshine in, but once inside, I longed for the familiar fresh air of the pond.

"Remember what I told you," Axel said in a quiet voice. "She is not the same Minna you knew. It is difficult to see, even for me. *Ja*, every time I come here, I say hello to the new Minna and good-bye to the old Minna."

"She couldn't have changed that much," I said.

Axel shook his head. "Hello-good-bye," he murmured.

We stepped into the elevator with a man who carried a vase of roses and sweet peas and baby's breath. When the doors closed, the elevator filled with the perfume of the blossoms. I had to stifle a laugh as I compared the bouquet of flowers to Axel's bouquet of bananas. Yes, Isabella, at first I thought it was comical. Then I realized Axel could have brought flowers, too. The very same blossoms bloomed in Minna's garden. But no, Axel had chosen fruit. And not even an exotic fruit. I shook my head in disgust. If I was ever going to learn about love, it wouldn't be from my family. They didn't know the first thing about it.

When the elevator door opened, it was the noise that reached me first—the sounds of many lives under one roof: two radios playing different stations, one end of a phone conversation, a cart rumbling down the hall. I hurried out of the elevator ahead of Axel. I'm sure he mistook my rushing for eagerness, Isabella, when in fact I was ashamed to be seen with him and his silly bouquet of bananas. I was the first to come upon room 302, Minna's room.

She sat in a sea blue chair, wearing a sea green dress.

Her hands were folded in front of her. When she saw me, she rubbed her hands together and folded them again.

"Minna!" I rushed to her side, my arms raised for a hug. Minna's expression stopped me.

She was looking through me, past me, to my uncle. "Axel?" she asked.

"*Ja.*"

"Hello, Axel!" Then she turned back to me and smiled politely. "And hello to you . . . dear."

Dear? I glanced sideways at Axel.

"Minna," said Axel. "This is Bitte Liten, your niece, come for a visit."

"How nice." Minna closed her eyes. I thought she was remembering. "Bitte Liten," she said to herself, as if she hadn't said it a thousand times before: *See the stars, Bitte. Bitte, I have cookies baking. Shall I sing, Bitte? Shall I sing your special lullaby?*

"Bitte Liten," Minna said again. "Such an unusual name. A Norwegian phrase, isn't it?"

"Yes," I said. "Norwegian."

"My husband is Norwegian, you know. My Axel."

"I know," I began. "Axel's my—"

"So nice of you to come, dear. So very nice." Minna refolded her hands and licked her lips. I followed her gaze to Axel's bananas. She was more interested in those bananas than in me, Isabella.

When Axel held them out for her, Minna's eyes sparkled. "Well, what is this?" she asked in a delighted voice.

"For you," said Axel gallantly. He stepped forward to present his bouquet.

"For me?"

"*Ja.*" Axel bowed. "A gift."

Minna took the bananas and set them in her lap. She reached up with her other hand and touched Axel's cheek. "Oh, Axel," she said, "*bananas.*"

She broke one from the bunch and carefully peeled the skin in four equal flaps. She took a delicate bite. "Mmm," she said. "It's perfect. A perfect banana, Axel."

"Only the best for my Minna," Axel said proudly.

When she had finished, she looked at me again. "Where are my manners?" she said. She held up the rest of her bananas. "Would you like one . . . dear?"

"Minna," Axel reminded her, "this is your niece, Bitte Liten, come for a visit."

"Bitte Liten," said Minna. "Such an unusual name. A Norwegian phrase, isn't it?" She continued to hold the bananas out for me. "Please have one."

"No, thank you," I said. "I'm not really hungry." It was true, Isabella. I couldn't have forced the smallest bite past the lump in my throat. I tried to swallow. If only my Minna would recognize me, the lump would go away. Suddenly I bent down and wrapped my arms around her. Surely if she felt my hug, she would know me. "Minna," I said. "It's me!"

Minna sat stiffly until I let her go.

That day I discovered a sadness beyond crying, Isabella. I had never felt such a sadness before that moment. Then anger pushed the sadness aside. I wanted to shake Minna, to shout at her. How could she have forgotten everything? How could she have forgotten *me?*

I must have been looking fiercely at her because Minna's face crumpled. She had that terrible question in her eyes again. My anger changed to nervousness because I knew for certain Minna was going to put words to her terrible question.

"Can you tell me something . . . dear?" she asked.

When I nodded, she clutched my hand. "Can you tell me how? How did I get here?"

I relaxed. "That's easy, Minna. From the pond, you cross the bridge at Danfarr, get on the freeway, take Exit 109, go west on Washington, right at the bank, left at the church, and right again onto Willow Avenue."

Minna let go of my hand. Her eyes looked even more puzzled. "No," she said. "I mean, how did I *get* here?"

"Ohhh," I said. Oh. I couldn't have put it into words

exactly, but I knew then that Minna was not speaking of a trip to the city. She was speaking of a different kind of journey. The kind where you don't take a suitcase. The kind where you look in the mirror one day and see yourself at a certain place in your life, but you don't know how it happened, or when. In that case, I was as lost as Minna.

"I guess I don't know," I said truthfully. "I guess I don't know how you got here."

"You have been ill, Minna," Axel explained. "We have talked about this. Remember?"

I could see Minna didn't remember those talks any more than she remembered me. She looked at her lap. Her eyes widened in surprise. "Bananas?" she asked, and she was delighted all over again.

"*Ja,* for you," Axel said gently. "All for you." He kissed Minna on the forehead. I patted her sea green sleeve.

"Good-bye," we said.

"Mmm," said my favorite aunt, smiling at her bananas.

Axel and I were quiet as we walked away from Minna. We stayed quiet as we stood in the elevator, waiting for the door to close. I kept my eyes down so Axel wouldn't see my tears. I looked at his hands. Empty of bananas, they seemed too big for his body.

This is what I wondered, Isabella: on a journey

without a suitcase, where do you carry your most precious belongings?

From the hallway came the noise—the sounds of many lives under one roof. I heard a television and a squeaky wheelchair and singing. Singing? Yes, Isabella, a sweet croaky voice singing, "*I see the moon. The moon sees me. The moon sees the one . . .*"

The elevator door shut with a whoosh.

Axel's too-big hand moved to take my hand. "Ah," he whispered. "She carries you in her heart."

Chapter Seven

THE FUTURE

On the drive back to the pond, I thought about the Minna I had once known, the Minna who remembered my name. I wished I could go back in time, but I knew I couldn't. We move through life in one direction, Isabella.

"Are you all right?" Axel asked gently.

I shrugged. I couldn't put my feelings into words. I looked out the window. Our big car cast a shadow against the roadside. I guess I could have told Axel the new Minna seemed like a shadow of the old Minna. I guess I could have told him I loved the shadow because I loved the one who cast it. But how could I have explained how it felt to hug that shadow?

"Mamma didn't tell me it was this bad," I said.

"She didn't know," Axel said. "She has been so worried about Kari, I didn't want to add to her troubles."

Of course, I thought. Kari again. "Will Minna ever get better?"

Axel shook his head slowly. "*Nei.* As I understand it, she will forget more and more until there is only the present for her. Then Minna will live in the exact *now.*"

At first that didn't sound so awful, Isabella. If you didn't remember the past, you wouldn't have to feel bad about losing it. If you didn't think about the future, you wouldn't have to worry about living through it. But another side of me knew that memories and dreams were two important parts of life. Someday Minna would lose them both. And then what? Would even the shadow of Minna disappear?

I glanced at Axel, my Norwegian uncle. I wondered how he felt, every visit saying "hello" and "good-bye." Was it harder on him than on Minna? How would I ever know? Could I ask her? *Minna, how does it feel to be a shadow?* No, of course not. But except for her terrible question, she seemed happy enough. I pictured her eyes when she tasted Axel's bananas. "Radiant" is how Claire's magazines would have described Minna's eyes. I guessed then that Axel knew something Claire's magazines couldn't tell him: yes, Axel knew what Minna needed.

I stared at my uncle's battle-weary face. Sunlight caught in his hair. "Axel," I said slowly, "I've been thinking about those bananas. You're like a Viking hero bringing treasures to your sweetheart."

Axel blinked, waving my thought away with his hand. "*Nei,*" he said. "Not I."

I touched his arm. "Yes, you."

We sailed on in silence, letting our tears flow for Minna and for the journey she had taken without us and for our own sad journey ahead.

When we arrived at the cabin, Axel changed into his overalls and retreated to Minna's garden. I pulled on my bathing suit and escaped to the water. The pond shimmered. I floated on my back, my mind full of questions with no answers. The water soothed me. I pressed my fingers to my throat and felt the pulsing of my Viking blood. Like the Vikings, I was drawn to the water. And so I swam every day, sometimes twice a day.

When I wasn't swimming, I filled my time in other ways. I weeded Minna's garden. I swept every corner of the house. I dusted and polished, watered and raked. And I visited Minna with my uncle Axel. I baked her a batch of raisin cookies. I helped Axel pick out perfect banana bunches. One lazy afternoon I lulled Minna to sleep by singing the moon song over and over, humming between verses the way she had done for me when I was a little girl and I couldn't get to sleep.

We seemed to be trading places, Minna and I, until

I felt more like the aunt than the niece. I didn't mind taking care of Minna, Isabella. Really, I didn't. But after two weeks at the pond, I began to wish there were someone to take care of me.

One morning, I clipped roses the way Minna used to do. I put the roses in a vase on the entryway table.

"Lovely," Axel said.

"Thanks." I shrugged. I did these little things, Isabella, because I couldn't change the big things: Axel's loneliness, Minna's forgetfulness, your future.

I did the little things and time passed.

At first I wanted it to pass quickly, to bring me closer to going home. Mamma had said I could come home after you were born. But home would be different then. Everything would be different. I didn't want to think about it. I decided I wanted time to pass slowly, so Minna wouldn't disappear, so I wouldn't have to grow up and face more changes.

But the sun kept rising in the morning and setting in the evening, and the days passed whether I wanted them to or not.

On some of those days, I got mail. Nothing from Claire, but quick notes from Pappa, crop updates from Jorgen, three care packages from Mamma.

And on my eighteenth day at Axel's, my uncle called me in from the pond. "Telephone!" he shouted.

Isabella has come, I thought. And Isabella has gone.

My stomach clenched tight. Your birth—the very thing I had looked forward to since winter—was going to be the thing that would take you away from me. Somehow I had been able to ignore that fact. Now I stumbled on the path, dizzy with the thought.

"Is it time? Is the baby . . . on her way?" I waited breathlessly for Axel's answer.

"*Nei,* but it is your sister calling."

Kari's voice sounded far away. "I was just thinking about you, Bitte. I was wondering how you were doing at the pond, with Minna gone and everything."

"It's not so bad," I said. "Really, it's not. Axel's here." And as I said those words, I realized how true they were. Axel was there, taking care of me. "But it's not like it used to be," I told Kari. "I wish you could be here." I wished a lot of things, Isabella.

"Me, too," Kari said. "I miss you. I miss the way things used to be." Then she was quiet for so long, Isabella, I began to wonder if she had forgotten why she had called.

"Would you do me a favor, Bitte?" Kari asked finally.

"Sure," I said. "What?"

"Will you try to understand? Will you try to put yourself in my shoes?"

I thought of Kari's blue thongs, flip-flopping across the porch, her feet swelling against the straps in the summer heat. I was going to ask why she cared what I thought, but I sensed from the sound of her faraway voice how important it was to her. "All right," I said reluctantly. "I'll try."

I was still light-headed from my startling, stumbling trip up the path. "When you first called," I said, "I thought the baby had already been born. I thought she had already gone with . . . those people. And that I hadn't even gotten to see her. I'd sure like to see her." I waited for Kari to invite me back home, to be a part of the family again. When she didn't, I realized that would be Mamma's decision. I asked, carefully, "Will you get to see the baby?"

"Oh yes," Kari said softly. "I'll see her. Or him. I have it all planned out."

After another long silence we said good-bye, the way you do when the conversation isn't finished but the talking is done.

"All is well?" Axel said when I hung up the phone.

I nodded. "I guess so. Kari asked me to try to understand." I wiggled my bare toes against the cool of the hallway floor. "I don't know why she cares. She's going to do what she wants anyway. She already made her plans without me. They all did. They left me out, like always."

"*Ja*, they left you out and then you left yourself out."

"What do you mean?" Axel talked as if being sent to the pond was my idea, Isabella.

"I mean, when Kari tried to make you part of her plan, you refused, didn't you?"

"Well, no one even asked me about my plans. All they ever talked about were Kari's feelings, Kari's dreams, Kari's plans."

"For?" Axel waited.

"For the baby."

"Whose baby?"

I looked at my feet. "Kari's," I mumbled. "Kari's baby."

"*Ja.*" Axel patted my shoulder. "Maybe you *could* try to understand, Bitte."

I did try, Isabella. I sat on the guest bed that very afternoon, thinking if I were in Kari's shoes, I would take care of my baby myself. I would get married, even though I didn't want to, even though it wouldn't last. I would live in a small house with roses in the garden, and I wouldn't let weeds grow there.

I didn't plan to rest, Isabella, but when I sank back against Minna's soft comforter, I fell into a sound sleep. I slept for the whole afternoon, and I dreamed of you.

I dreamed we were in the nightstand drawer, sleeping on tiny mouse-mattress beds. You asked if I was a baby, too, and I said something like, "No, I'm twelve, old enough to take care of you myself. Me. Auntie Me. Myself." So you said, "Auntie Me, I'm hungry."

I started to tell you about all the things we were going to do together.

"I'm hungry," you said.

I promised to show you the night sky.

"I'm hungry," you said.

I handed you a bouquet of roses and baby's breath and sweet peas.

"I'm hungry."

I didn't have any food, Isabella, not even a banana, but I told you my dreams for your fairy-tale future.

All you said was, "I'm hungry." Your voice sounded weak. It was scary. I could hear my heart pounding softly, then louder, louder, louder, like a giant clock tick-tocking the seconds away, bringing us all closer to the future.

"Hungry," you said. "Hungry."

Chapter Eight

VIKING BLOOD

"Bitte!" Axel's voice cut through my dream. He knocked on the guest-room door. Thump-*thump*. Thump-*thump*. Thump-*thump*.

"Bitte! Are you hungry?"

I *was* hungry, and happy to leave my dream behind. Axel's steamed fish and potatoes filled a space I hadn't known was empty.

We stayed later than usual at the pond that night. It was a clear night, Isabella, and the sky was full of stars.

"I wanted to teach Kari's baby about the stars," I told Axel, "the way Minna taught me." Maybe it wasn't what you needed, Isabella. After all, you couldn't eat the stars. But I was remembering Minna, pointing out the constellations, especially the one constellation that had taken me so long to see. "It makes me sad to think I won't be able to show the baby the Little Bear."

Axel held his hands so the firelight flickered against his palms. "*Ja*, but someone will be there to show her. Someone like Minna, who always wanted a child. That is something to be happy about."

Was it? I wondered. Then why didn't I feel happy?

"I wonder if a person like me could ever find all the constellations," I said.

Axel stoked the fire. "At one time, you could not find the Little Bear, *ja*?"

"Well, it didn't look like a little bear," I complained. "It looked like a square with a tail."

"Right," said Axel. "That was what made it hard to find, I think. You were expecting it to look like your idea of a bear, and it didn't."

I frowned, remembering my frustration. Then I smiled. "Once I saw the Little Bear, I never forgot what it looked liked."

"*Stjerner*," Axel said slowly. "Stars. We connect them into groups and patterns, but they are still separate. Each star in the constellation has its own name. Did you know that? Each star has its own identity."

Then stars are like people in a family, I thought. Separate but connected. The people in our family seemed more separate than connected that summer.

Minna once told me the distance between stars was measured in light years. That's how I felt, Isabella, light years away from everyone but Axel. Would our family ever be connected again?

Early the next morning, as I floated in the pond, I remembered a time we had all splashed together under the summer sun—Pappa, Axel, Jorgen, Mamma, Minna, Kari, and I. In those days, Mamma would bury her face in my hair after the sun had dried it. Later she bathed me in the kitchen sink. Still later, after Minna had sung me to sleep, Mamma would slip into the guest room and I would wake to find her standing over the bed. I could feel her smiling in the dark, Isabella.

It was a memory that made me happy, yes, but also sad and tired. I swam to shore, weighed down with a dull heaviness.

Back in the guest room, I dried off with a fluffy towel. I slipped into a pair of underpants and my giant white T-shirt.

The next thing I did surprised me. Some might call it curiosity, Isabella. Some might call it doing what my sister, Kari, had asked me to do. But I believe I was pulled, like the tides are pulled by the moon. I believe I was pulled to the album of Jacob and Hope.

Did they know what you needed?

I settled onto the guest bed and opened the album. I studied the photographs and read the captions Hope and Jacob had written.

—We live in a family neighborhood with a good school nearby and lots of other children to play with.
—Our home is a comfortable place with a wonderful garden . . .
—strawberries, blueberries and raspberries to pick . . .
—birds and squirrels and bugs to watch . . .
—a patio just right for tricycle riding . . .
—and two lovable cats supervising it all.

I smiled against my will. I had to admit, Isabella, it sounded nice.

Had Kari also been enchanted by the garden? I wondered, or had she been looking at the other words Hope and Jacob had written: faith, education, communication.

My own favorite part was at the end:

—We have arms for hugging, laps for cuddling, ears for listening, and a full cookie jar.

I was beginning to understand.

Hope and Jacob could feed you when you were hungry. More than that, they could give you the kind of life Kari wanted you to have. Under a photograph of a nursery filled with toys and clothes and empty picture frames, they had written, "We have many dreams for our child." I nodded. We all had dreams for you, Isabella, just different characters playing the part of parents.

I didn't want to feel good about Hope and Jacob, but I wanted to let Kari know that I had looked at the album, that I had tried to put myself in her shoes. I found a postcard in Minna's old desk. I wrote, "Strawberries, raspberries, and blueberries. Mmmmmm. A full cookie jar. Yummy."

As I slipped the postcard into Axel's mailbox, I thought of Hope and Jacob and Kari. Of all the people in the world, they had somehow found each other. I got goose bumps thinking of that. It seemed astonishing, Isabella, that these three people with the same dream had found each other. But I did not want to be astonished. I rubbed away the goose bumps. I closed myself in the guest room, curled up on the bed, and squeezed my eyes shut tight.

Trying to understand Kari's decision was making me uncomfortable. I felt a nervousness low in my stomach. The same nervousness I associated with seeing the new Minna and losing the old one. The same heaviness I'd felt remembering Mamma smiling in the dark. But I wasn't thinking about Minna or Mamma that morning. No, I was thinking about me.

It looked like you would be happy, Isabella. Jacob and Hope would be happy, too. But what about me? I wrapped Minna's comforter around me like a cocoon and fell asleep asking, What about me, me, me, me, me?

I dreamed of you again. Here is what I remember of it: We were small, like before, sleeping on our mouse mattresses. Kari was there. "Laps for cuddling," she squeaked. "Ears for listening."

Hope appeared. I wanted her to go away. "Ma-ma," you said. You raised your arms to Hope. She picked you up and held you close. Kari sat on the bed beside me. "Arms for hugging," she squeaked. Her own arms hung empty. And this was the strangest part of the dream, Isabella. At that moment, I became Kari. Yes. For one split second, Kari's empty arms belonged to me. A sharp pain shot through me. Then, just as suddenly, the pain passed in a white heat. I was me again.

I'd never had such a dream. I felt stunned, Isabella. In a daze, I sat up on the edge of my mouse mattress. I felt warm all over and damp where I was sitting.

I realized I wasn't dreaming anymore. I opened my eyes and found myself sitting on the edge of Minna's guest bed. Still warm. Still damp.

I headed for Minna's powder room, scolding myself

the whole way there: You're just like a big baby, Bitte, wetting your pants at a strange dream.

But I hadn't wet my pants, Isabella. I will share this private thing with you. The dampness was a crimson-colored stripe.

I was a woman.

Oh, Isabella, what a relief to see there wasn't much blood. I blew out a long breath and then another. I was afraid and excited and confused, all at the same time. My pulse throbbed. What should I do? Who could I turn to?

Minna would have helped me, but she wasn't there. I could hear Axel hoeing rocks in the garden. I shook my head. No, not a man! He wouldn't understand. I went to the hall phone and dialed long distance.

"Claire!" I said, when she answered. "It's me!"

"Bitte! I miss you!" Claire said.

"Guess what?" I whispered.

"What?" Claire whispered back.

"I had my . . . I started . . . I guess you'd say I'm a woman!" I announced. "Just today. Just now!"

"Really? Well, it's about time!" Claire said. "Hey! I saw Robert McCormick at the swimming pool yester-day. His hair is beginning to bleach out and he has muscles!" Claire chatted on as if my news were noth-ing. "He's handsome, Bitte. Handsome! You won't be-lieve it till you see it for yourself. I think I'm in love. I mean, I know he gave you your first kiss. But this is True Love, Bitte."

True Love. I sighed. Robert McCormick seemed from another life, and in a way, so did Claire. "I'd better go now," I said. "This is long distance."

"Okay. Wish me luck with Robert." Claire made kissing noises into the phone just before I pressed the button to cut off our connection.

I dialed again.

Someday you will become a woman, Isabella. You will be officially grown up and at the same time, you will be like a little girl. You will want to talk to someone who understands. Someone who knows everything about you—the smell of your hair after a day in the sun, the feel of soap sliding over your skin, the sound of your breathing in the middle of the night.

Maybe, like me, you will be away from home the day you become a woman. Maybe you will dial the phone and hear it ringing once, twice, seven times. And just before you start to hang up, you will pray, "*Answer*. Please answer. I need you, Mamma."

Chapter Nine

THE LAST
MOUSE BED

I sat alone in Axel's hallway, listening to Mamma's phone ringing across the miles. I thought about how important it is to have someone on the other end of the line. *Seven* rings, *eight, nine, ten* . . .

"Hello?" Mamma's voice.

"Mamma! It's me!" I searched my mind for the right words. "Mamma, I'm a woman today."

Mamma gave out a little gasp. "Ah! My Bitte?" Her voice sounded husky. "My beautiful, intelligent, independent daughter, now a young woman?"

I pulled back to look at the receiver. Was Mamma talking about me? She had never called me those things before: beautiful, intelligent, independent. I thought maybe that was what becoming a woman was all about, Isabella: people telling you things they wouldn't tell a child.

I heard Mamma take a deep breath and sigh. "I say hello to Bitte the young woman, but I don't want to say good-bye to Bitte the little girl."

Do we have to say good-bye, I wondered? Was Bitte, the girl, gone forever? I thought of my sister, waving from our front porch.

"How is Kari today?" I asked.

"Ah, she's uncomfortable. Ready for the baby to come. I think it will be any day." Mamma clicked her tongue. "My own two babies, both young women. I wish I could be in two places at one time, Bitte. You understand, don't you, that I have to stay with Kari? She needs us right now, more than you do, don't you think?"

"Yes, Mamma," I said, trying to behave like a grown-up. Trying to act like the woman I had just become. "I understand," I said. But a person can understand something, Isabella, and still not like it.

Then Mamma said briskly, "Do you know what to do?"

"Yes, Mamma. I know what to do." After all, I'd had Claire, and I'd had health class.

But Mamma explained anyway, which is what I had been hoping for. Her cool, clear instructions washed away my fears. "All set?" she asked, when she was finished.

"All set," I said.

"Good then. I'd like to talk to your Uncle Axel, please. But first, I want to say thank you for calling, Bitte. Thank you for including me in this important day."

I hugged the phone to my ear. "Isn't that what families are for, Mamma?"

I waved Axel in from the garden. While he was talking with Mamma, I went back into the guest room. Mamma's words were still fresh in my mind.

I opened the nightstand drawer and pulled out the last mouse bed. I set aside the tiny quilt and the knitted blanket and little fitted sheet. Underneath it all was the mouse mattress that wasn't really a mattress at all, but a clean white pad.

I carefully folded the quilt and the blanket and the sheet and shut them away in the drawer.

"Good-bye," I said softly.

I carried the pad into Minna's powder room. There, I followed Mamma's instructions. Sooner or later, I thought, I'll have to ask Axel to take me to the store for more supplies. I frowned. I'd have to make up a reason for going. The real reason was much too private. I remembered then the summer Kari had not wanted to bring the mouse mattresses out in the open. Her reaction didn't seem so confusing anymore.

I took a deep breath that turned into a yawn. The nervous pain was gone, but I felt drowsy again. I wandered in and lay on Minna's guest bed. Just before I dozed off, I heard Axel's big car engine race to a start.

No dreams this time, Isabella. I slept hard, and when I woke, it was evening and Axel had returned. I don't know if it was his soft knocking that woke me or the delicious smells drifting in from the kitchen.

"Bitte," said Axel, "will you join me by the pond?"

"In a minute," I mumbled. I felt much better after my rest. I quickly dressed and combed my hair and glanced in the mirror to see if I looked any different yet. Would Axel be able to tell I had become a woman? No. I was relieved to see that on the outside, I was still the same Bitte.

In the kitchen, Axel handed me a basket. "If you will carry this, please, I will meet you at the pond."

The basket was heavy. Once at the pond, I set our dinner out on the cloth Axel had packed on top. Beneath it were warm dishes filled with roasted chicken and boiled potatoes and tiny asparagus spears. I was surprised when I pulled good china and silverware from the bottom of the basket. I was even more surprised to find, tucked in the corner, a small bottle of wine.

"It's a feast!" I called eagerly to Axel, as he walked toward me. In one hand, he carried two of Minna's crystal goblets. In the other, one of her rosebuds, just starting to open.

He knelt down to pour the wine, a full goblet for himself and a splash of red for me. Picture this, Isabella: evening sunlight shining through ruby-colored wine, making it glow beautiful as stained glass.

I took the goblet Axel offered. He handed me the rosebud as well. "Minna would want to be in on the celebration," he said.

"Celebration?"

"*Ja.*" Axel raised his glass. "To you."

My face flamed red as the wine, I'm sure. Imagine, Isabella. Mamma had told him! I needed to busy myself in that awkward moment. I brought Minna's crystal to my lips and took a sip. A warm thrill went through me. A thrill of shyness and pride.

Axel began serving the dinner. "Eat!" he said. "Enjoy!" He spoke no more about celebrations. But every time I sipped my wine, I experienced the toast to my womanhood, and the same shy, proud thrill.

Axel and I talked about Minna and cooking and school until the moon began to rise. I thought it was a full moon, but Axel said, "Not quite."

He stared at the moon for a long time. Then he poured himself more wine.

"You're a good cook," I said.

"*Takk,*" Axel said. "Thank you." He patted his mouth

with his napkin. "In the old days in Norway, before my time and my grandfather's time and my grandfather's grandfather's time, the women did all the cooking."

"Mamma still does all the cooking," I said. Then I realized Axel was not making conversation. He was introducing a story.

"In the old days in Norway, when their sons and husbands readied themselves for a voyage, the women prepared food to take along. There was nowhere to cook on the longships, so the Vikings ate cold food when their journey took them across the seas. *Nei*, not much extra space on a Viking ship. No separate rooms. They slept in sleeping bags made of reindeer skins. The women sewed the sleeping bags, creating a warm place to rest. *Ja*, the women provided what was needed to survive on a journey to the shores of a new land."

Axel stopped talking to sip his wine.

"Can you imagine the preparations, Bitte? And the excitement of the coming voyage? The laying in of food and clothing and every other thing a person would need to stay alive? Readying the holds of the ship for the journey, so when the seas raged on the outside, the sailors would be secure on the inside.

"The women," Axel said, "lining the longships."

I *could* imagine it, Isabella. I could almost hear them singing as they went about their work.

Axel cleared his throat. "Sometimes the voyages were called off. No one went aboard ship after all, so there was no one to keep snug and safe. Then would come the unloading of all that would have kept the sailors alive. Unloading until the longship stood empty once more and ready for the next voyage."

Axel was silent for a very long time.

"And?" I asked.

"And?" he asked back.

"Is that the end?"

Axel smiled. "*Nei*. It is only the beginning."

"The beginning?" I wondered why Axel was speaking in riddles.

He looked to the stars. "Sonja," he mumbled with a shrug, "it's the best I can do."

Sonja was Mamma's name. I decided too much red wine had affected Axel's thinking, so I didn't ask any more questions that night. I never forgot his peculiar story, though. Years later, it made sense to me. The full longship was like a woman's body, making ready for a child, the way Kari's body had prepared itself for you, Isabella. And the loading and unloading of the longship, the cycle of filling and emptying—that had been *my* part of the story. Poor Axel had been trying to tell me the tale of becoming a woman the only way he knew how—through his Viking lore.

But when I was twelve, Isabella, it was just a story with no middle and no end, only a beginning. A mysterious beginning.

As I got ready to go to sleep the night of our celebration, I thought of the reindeer-skin sleeping bags. Those Viking beds reminded me of my little mouse bed. I opened the nightstand drawer looking for the bedclothes. Instead, I found the drawer filled with mouse mattresses, just like in the days of Minna.

Axel, I thought. Axel bought these and put them here. My face flamed again. But I was grateful, too, for not having to ask.

These are not for playing anymore, I told myself. Things are different now. I'm different. But I didn't feel different, Isabella. I had expected to suddenly change on the day I became a woman, to want to read bridal magazines or bake pies for farmhands or waltz in the wheat fields with a shy, handsome boy. I had expected, on the day I became a woman, to become like the women I knew—Claire, Kari, Minna, Mamma. But I was not any of those women. I was me. And I wanted to play.

I reached for the tiny fitted sheet. I slipped it onto a brand-new mouse mattress.

"Hello," I said softly, and smiled.

Chapter Ten

FULL MOON

Two days after my celebration, I came out to the kitchen to find Axel hidden behind the morning newspaper. He had set a glass of orange juice at my place.

"*God morgen,* Bitte." His voice came from behind the paper. "Full moon tonight. It will be today, I think."

"What will be today?"

"*Lille* Kari," Axel said. "Little Kari's journey. And the baby's, too. One journey coming to an end. One just beginning."

Axel was talking about you coming into the world, Isabella. You. I sat down slowly. Could it really be so close to happening? What would you look like? Sound like? Smell like? How would your skin feel? I'd never know. I hoped maybe Axel was mistaken about the timing. If you weren't born yet, you could still live in my imagination. I guess I wanted you to be my make-believe baby forever.

"What does the full moon have to do with it?" I asked.

"I see it in the paper every month," Axel said. "Full moon. A few days later, a long list of newborns. It makes sense. If the moon can rule the tides, it can surely nudge a baby."

Was this true? I wondered. If it were true, Isabella, and not one of Axel's Norwegian tales, then you *would* be here soon. My heart beat faster at the thought.

"Ah, brave Kari. *Lille modige* Kari." Axel brought the paper down and lifted his eyebrows at me. "Toast?"

I raised my glass of orange juice. "To Kari," I said. "To Kari and her baby."

Axel chuckled and raised his own glass. "To life," he said, and chuckled again.

"Why are you laughing?" I asked. "What's the joke?"

"I was just wondering if you wanted some toast. To eat."

I giggled. "Oh!" I got up and busied myself at the counter, filling the kitchen with the smells of toasting bread and melted butter. I set a neat stack in the middle of the table and poured myself a half mug of coffee. Mamma wasn't there to stop me. Besides, I was a young woman, wasn't I?

Sitting across from Axel once more, I stirred cream into my coffee. I dipped into the sugar bowl and stared at the crystals falling from my spoon. Suddenly I ached for my family. I missed them—Mamma, Pappa, Jorgen, and Kari. I missed our morning conversations. I missed the smell of rhubarb pie bubbling in the oven and the sound of wheat whispering through the open windows.

Not that I hadn't enjoyed my days with my uncle Axel. Not at all, Isabella. I had never really known him before, and now I did. I liked the way he treated me, the way he called my sister *modig*. Brave.

But I wanted to be with Kari and the rest of my family. It seemed to me the hardest part of Kari's journey was yet to come, and I ached to be there, Isabella, to welcome you into the world. But I had been sent away, and I hadn't been asked home again.

I drank my coffee, but I hardly tasted it, I was so restless with waiting for news of you.

At four o'clock that afternoon, I was kneeling in the garden when I heard the phone ring. The next I knew, Axel stood before me with his car keys dangling from his fingers. "Let's go for a drive," he said, with a crooked smile.

"The baby?"

"On its way."

"And we're going?"

Axel nodded.

I ran to the house, washed, packed, and returned to the car in less than ten minutes, Isabella. After I caught my breath, I asked, "Was that Mamma on the phone?"

"*Ja.*"

"What did she say?"

"She said, 'We're heading for the hospital right now.' She said, 'Kari wants Bitte to be there.'"

"She got my postcard!"

"*Ja.*"

"But what about Mamma?"

"She said"—Axel paused—"'Can Bitte do it?'"

"Do what?"

"Can Bitte let go? Can Bitte let Kari let go?" Axel opened the car door for me. "Your Mamma said, 'Don't bring her if she can't do it.'"

"And what did you say?"

"I'm bringing you, aren't I?" Axel watched me get in the car. He closed the door behind me and came around to the driver's side. Once he was behind the wheel, he said, "Ah, Bitte, you love your sister. You love this baby. You want what is best for both of them. I know you do, even though what is best may break your heart, *ja?*"

"*Ja,*" I whispered.

Axel started the engine while I hugged my arms to

my chest. If my heart was not breaking, it was surely bending in two. Could I really let you go without a word, Isabella?

I didn't know. I only knew I was headed home to my family, where I belonged.

The drive would take four hours. We wouldn't get to the hospital until after eight o'clock. I drummed my fingers on the vinyl seat cover and tried to fill the time with conversation.

"The baby—do you think she's here yet?" I asked.

"Probably not," Axel said. "These things take time." He glanced at me. "What makes you think the baby is a she?"

"Maybe I'm just wishing for a niece," I said, "to carry on the tradition." Actually, Isabella, it never occurred to me you might be a boy. A boy named Isabella? No, I never let the thought cross my mind.

"Girl. Boy. A baby is a baby," Axel said, "every one full of promise."

Full of someone's rose-trellis, raisin-cookie dreams, I thought. Dreams of morning sunlight shining into a crib. Dreams of sitting by a campfire, watching the stars. Dreams of pointing out constellations, making connections, being connected.

It was a long time before I spoke again. I leaned toward Axel. "Even if I never meet her—the baby, I mean—I'll still be her aunt, won't I?"

The car lurched. A crease divided Axel's forehead. "What, Bitte?"

"An aunt. I'll still be her aunt, in a way."

"*Ja,* Bitte. You'll still be her aunt. Sure."

I wished Axel would drive faster. I spoke more loudly over the rising noise of the engine. "Don't you want to get there before she's born, Axel? Don't you want to be there when it actually happens?"

Axel nodded, but then he frowned and shifted to a lower gear.

Hurry! I wanted to shout. Drive faster, not slower! Isabella's on her way! Kari needs me! Hurry!

Down the road, the lights of a diner flashed red and blue. "It's seven o'clock," Axel said. "Would you like to stop for dinner?"

"No!" I said. "Thanks, I mean. But no thanks."

We drove on, past the diner, past the gas station, past the last rest stop.

I willed the wheels to roll faster, Isabella. Were we ever going to get to the hospital? What if we missed it? How unfair it would be to miss your arrival now that Kari trusted me to be there. Now that Mamma was giving me a second chance.

That's what I was thinking when Axel's big new car rattled once, jerked twice, shivered, and stopped.

Axel coasted to the side of the road. He tried and tried to restart the engine, Isabella. He muttered in

Norwegian—sending prayers to heaven or instructions to the car, I'm not sure which. He got out and looked under the hood. More muttering. He made some adjustments. Still, the engine would not start.

"No use," he said sadly.

I looked up and down the shadowy road. "How far is it?" I asked. "Maybe we can walk."

Axel shook his head. "It's an hour's drive, Bitte. Too far to walk."

I reached for his hand. "Please, Axel," I said. "How else will we get there?"

We walked by the light of the sinking sun until our legs ached and our breathing came in deep gasps.

"Maybe . . . we could hitch . . . a ride," I suggested breathlessly.

Axel shook his head. "Too dangerous."

The few cars on the road sped past anyway, Isabella. No one seemed eager to pick up an old man and a tired young woman.

I wish someone would stop, I thought. I remembered Mamma telling me once, "Be careful what you wish for, Bitte. It might come true." I wished harder.

We saw the headlights first. Headlights coming toward us, slowing down, passing us by. We whirled around to see a battered-looking truck. It turned and began to creep slowly back to us.

Be careful what you wish for, I thought again. The hairs on my neck prickled when I saw crates stacked in the open bed of the truck. My imagination went wild. What were in those crates? Or who . . . ?

Axel looked worried, too, but suddenly he beamed and pointed to the side of the truck. "Gunnarsen's," he read.

"Hello, Mr. Gunnarsen!" Axel greeted the driver. I recognized the owner of the roadside fruit stand where we had stopped on our way to see Minna.

"Hello, my friend," Mr. Gunnarsen answered. "I was doing business in town today. I'm on my way home now to set up for morning market. When I saw you, I thought, Could that be Axel, my most selective customer, walking along the road at this hour? What could he be doing? I thought."

After Axel explained, Mr. Gunnarsen told us he was sorry he had no room for passengers in his front seat. But he kindly cleared a space for us in the back of his truck.

And so, Isabella, we rode to the hospital with the wind in our hair and the sweet smell of fruit surrounding us. Crates and crates of fruit: grapes, peaches, melons and yes, bananas—the fruit of love.

It was nearly nine o'clock when Mr. Gunnarsen let us off at the hospital entrance. Axel put his arm around my shoulder. I prayed we hadn't missed the beginning of your journey. I wanted to run through the doorway, but Axel held me back. "Turn around," he said. "Look."

Above the horizon, the moon was rising, golden orange and full of promise.

Chapter Eleven

WELCOME HOME

I saw Pappa and Jorgen before they saw me. They sat together in the small waiting room. When Jorgen heard my running footsteps, he looked up and called out happily, "Little Bitte!"

Pappa wrapped me in a bear hug. It had been three weeks since I had seen my brother and my father, since we had played the what-does-the-wheat-say? game. It seemed like a lifetime. Pappa's arms felt warm and strong around me. We stood back and smiled at each other. When I saw his eyes crinkle, I knew I was home, Isabella. I wasn't in my house, but I was home.

"Where's Mamma?" I asked.

"In the delivery room with Kari," Jorgen said.

"How is she?"

"Kari's fine. I don't know about Mamma, though. She looks more tired every time she gives us a progress report. But she also looks more excited." Jorgen chuckled.

I heard an answering chuckle and a soft laugh from across the room. I looked over Pappa's shoulder. Was I dreaming? No, Isabella. The people from Kari's photo album were standing right in front of me.

Hope and Jacob had come to life.

I felt a punch of surprise in my stomach. What were *they* doing here?

Jacob was rolling and unrolling a sports magazine. Hope held a book of baby names. She wasn't reading though. She was staring back at me.

I leaned closer to Pappa.

"You must be Bitte," Hope said.

Pappa stood, and guided me forward. "Hope, Jacob, I'd like to introduce our younger daughter. Bitte, this is . . . these are . . . the parents."

I crossed my arms over my chest.

Axel cleared his throat.

I uncrossed my arms. But again I wondered, What are they *doing* here?

Jacob must have seen the shock on my face. "Your sister asked us to be here," he explained.

"I know it's unusual," Hope added. "We had no idea it was even possible. But here we are." Hope looked as surprised as I felt. "It's really special to be included this way. But then Kari's a special girl, isn't she?"

I nodded slowly, afraid to find out what other special surprises Kari had planned.

"Anyway, we're so glad to meet you, Bitte." Hope held out her hand. And do you know what, Isabella? It was warm. Jacob's hand was warm, too. Something inside me began to melt at the touch of their warm hands.

Warm hands would be good for changing your diapers. Good for rubbing your back. Good for holding on to when you took your first steps into the world.

I had never expected to meet Hope and Jacob in person. But now that I had met them and felt their warm hands, I couldn't stop staring. I had to make sure they were good enough for you, Isabella.

The first thing I noticed was that they seemed to belong together. Maybe it was because they touched a lot, as if they were telling each other, Everything is going to be okay.

She smelled like flowers. He smelled like baby oil and shampoo. I could tell he had shaved before coming to the hospital. Even though it was nighttime, he had shaved, all except his mustache.

Yes, Isabella, Jacob had a big bushy mustache. Claire once told me she thought a mustache made a man look like a sly fox. Claire was wrong. Jacob's mustache made him look like a friendly bear.

I studied their eyes. Hers were green and calm like

the pond on a sunny day. His were dancing pools of brown. And oh, Isabella, Jacob had crinkles! He had gentle wrinkles around his eyes, just like Pappa's.

Warm hands, crinkles, the smell of flowers. Those were my first impressions of Jacob and Hope.

Pappa was introducing them to Axel when Mamma walked into the room. Hope spun around eagerly.

"Not yet," Mamma told her, "but it's going well." She massaged one hand with the other. "That Kari has quite a grip. She's a strong one."

"Strong?" I repeated.

"Ah, there's my Bitte Liten." Mamma wrapped me in a hug, as Pappa had. Jorgen had been right. Up close, Mamma did look tired, but it was a good kind of tired, as if she'd been working hard in the garden, growing something beautiful.

"How are you, Sonja?" Axel asked.

"I'm fine," Mamma said. "Kari's the one doing all the work. All I do is lend her my hand to squeeze, and give her encouragement."

"She's lucky to have you for encouragement," said Hope. "Isn't that what mothers are for?"

Someone on the other end of the line, I thought, remembering my phone call.

"I'd better get back now." Mamma cupped my face in her hands. "I'm glad you decided to join us, Bitte."

"Tell Kari," I said.

Mamma nodded. "She'll be glad, too."

All our energy seemed to follow Mamma out of the waiting room. No one spoke. Not because there was so little to say, Isabella, but because there was so much, I think.

I studied the furniture, trying not to look anyone in the eye. I noticed a small flannel elephant on a chair in the corner. I picked it up and plucked at the ribbon tied around its neck. "Did you bring this?" I asked Jorgen.

"No."

"Pappa?"

"No."

"It's sweet." I looked at Hope and Jacob.

They shook their heads.

Pappa took a deep breath. "Angus brought it," he said, "but he couldn't stay to give it to the baby."

"*Ja*, I suppose we all have our limits," Axel said.

Pappa nodded, and I guessed they were speaking of Angus not being able to stay, not being able to bring himself to say hello and good-bye to you all in one breath.

Jorgen shook his head. "Strapping Angus, pale as bleached wheat."

Actually, all the men looked pale, Isabella. I thought of Kari, fighting to do all of this in her own way, and Mamma beside her, lending her strength, and Hope, standing guard like a scented soldier. Women can be strong, I thought, and men can be pale. Pale and gentle. What would Claire think of that?

I sat on the couch, stroking the elephant Angus had brought for you. Jacob sat down beside me. He, too, petted the elephant. "This will be very special to our baby someday, don't you think?"

I nodded. I liked the way he smiled at me when he said "our baby," Isabella, as if you belonged to us all.

Mamma came back twice more. "It will be a while," she said each time. Axel and I went to the cafeteria to eat. Later, we shared coffee and small talk with Jacob and Hope.

You can get to know people through small talk, Isabella. I know, now, that he laughs easily and she is the more serious one. That he doesn't always show his feelings, but she figures out what they are. That they waited a very long time for a child and that the waiting was hard.

"I learned how to wait," Hope said, "but I never learned how to like it."

I was getting tired of waiting myself. It was after midnight. I had already leafed through all the old magazines.

"Would you like to look at this?" Hope offered me her name book. She didn't know I already called you by name. And I didn't suggest *Isabella* to her. I hope you don't mind, but I wanted to keep that part of you for myself.

"Have you chosen a name?" Axel asked politely.

Hope shook her head. "Picking a name is a lot harder than I thought it would be." She turned to me. "A name should fit, don't you think?"

I shrugged. "My name means tiny, but I keep getting bigger and bigger."

Jacob laughed his easy laugh. "We're looking for a name that means curious, kind, exuberant"—he ticked off the qualities on his fingers—"courageous, gentle, thoughtful, strong, compassionate, loving, wise..." He put his hand on Hope's shoulder. "Did I leave anything out?" he teased.

"Happy," Hope said softly. She turned to me again. "Do you know what I mean by happy, Bitte? Not the leaping, laughing-out-loud kind of happy, but a deep-down kind of contentment." She blushed. "Do you know what I mean?"

"I think I do," I said. "But would you rather have a happy boy or a happy girl?"

"A baby is a baby," said Jacob, and Hope nodded her agreement.

That's what Axel had said, Isabella. But I'd had my heart set on a niece for so long. I frowned. Why did it matter? I wasn't going to get to know you anyway. Kari's plans hadn't included Auntie Me.

As if he suspected what I was thinking, Jacob said, "I really admire Kari."

Hope nodded. "I do, too. Your sister had everything so well planned out. She says she wants us to be the first to hold the baby"—she gave an astonished look to Jacob—"because we're the parents."

I flinched. Isn't it strange, Isabella, how the same exact words can bring such joy to one person and such pain to another? Hope and Jacob would get to hold you first. But would Kari get to hold you? Would Mamma? Would Pappa? I was almost afraid to wonder—would I?

If only . . . , I started to think, just as Mamma appeared at the door.

Her face glowed, Isabella. My dreams for a niece disappeared in that glow. Why? Because all I wanted at that moment was news of you. Girl. Boy. I didn't care which. A baby *was* a baby.

Mamma marched straight to Hope and Jacob. "Congratulations," she said. "You have a daughter."

I had expected all of us to jump up and down and shout and laugh and pound each other on the back, Isabella, the way you see it in the movies. But it was the other kind of happiness that filled the room. I saw it in Jacob's shining eyes and felt it in Hope's sudden squeeze—a quiet, deep-down content kind of happy.

Hope and Jacob hugged each other. Then Jacob

shook Pappa's hand and Jorgen's hand and Axel's hand. The men coughed and cleared their throats and turned away to wipe their eyes.

I watched it all with a singing heart: *Isabella! Isabella! You are here! Welcome! Welcome to the world!* It wasn't a time to think about the future or anything but the joy of your birth. The celebration of your life. Isabella's life. Isabella. You.

Hope hugged me again and then faced Mamma. They took each other's hands.

"A daughter," Hope said. The word seemed to hang in the hushed waiting room.

Daughter.

Mamma and Hope gazed at each other for a long time, their eyes filling with tears, their eyes saying so many things, I felt I was eavesdropping. And though I was a daughter and a woman, too, I backed away. Everyone backed away from Mamma and Hope, giving them their moment with each other. Pappa and Jorgen sank into the couch. Jacob patted the stuffed elephant. Axel looked out the window.

I waited and watched until Mamma and Hope were finished with their silent conversation. Until Mamma held out her arms to include Jacob as well as Hope. Until Mamma said, "Come. Meet your daughter."

Chapter Twelve

THE GIFT

You took my breath away.

I first saw you through the window of the hospital's rocking room. Your little face, less than an hour old, peeked out from your blanket. Even through the glass, you were more precious than any make-believe baby.

Kari did this, I thought. Kari brought this life into the world.

Hope cradled you. Jacob leaned over the back of her rocking chair to stare down at you. I could see right away that Hope and Jacob were your shelter, the way Mamma and Pappa were mine. I couldn't deny it, Isabella.

You were home.

You were home, and my sister, Kari, had helped you find your way there.

Hope and Jacob didn't see me watching through the

window, they were so intent on you. And no wonder, Isabella. You were their miracle. I slipped back to the waiting room before they noticed me.

Kari was dozing when we went to her room. I said hello and she opened her eyes. "You came," she said sleepily. "I'm glad."

"I'm glad, too," I said, as Kari's eyes closed again.

"It's late," Mamma reminded me, and it was. We all took one more peek at you as you slept soundly in your pink bassinet. Then we made our way home in the wee morning hours, all but Mamma who stayed by Kari's side. It was strange to be back in my room, strange and wonderfully familiar. I caught a glimpse of myself in the full-length mirror. Same room, different person, I thought. Maybe that was it. I went to sleep in my old bed and dreamed of your precious little face.

When the sun rose, it was still your birthday. You weren't even a day old, Isabella.

Mamma stayed with Kari most of the morning and went back again in the afternoon. The rest of us had to wait until after dinner to visit because, as Mamma told us, Kari needed time with you and time alone. Time to hold on, I thought to myself, and time to let go.

I didn't want to eat dinner. I wanted to get back to the hospital. But Mamma insisted. "We all need a decent meal before we go," she said. The grown-ups even ate slices of rhubarb pie.

I said, "None for me, thanks." My dessert would be meeting you, Isabella.

Regular visiting hours were over by the time we got to Kari's room. No one in the maternity ward seemed to mind, though. We talked quietly—Mamma, Pappa, Jorgen, Kari, Axel, and I.

Kari was in bed, the quilt she had made for you spread across her lap. She looked rested after her sleep. "The delivery wasn't so hard," she told us.

Mamma shook her head, remembering differently.

Kari smiled a modest smile. "Well, not as hard as I thought it would be."

"A girl," Jorgen said. "I suppose that means she'll be asking a lot of questions like a certain little Bitte I know."

Kari looked from Jorgen to me. "I suppose."

I rolled my eyes. What kind of questions would a newborn baby ask? I could only think of one. It was Minna's question: *How did I get here?* I started thinking Minna's terrible question wouldn't be so terrible if she knew the answer, Isabella.

Kari squinted at the wall clock. "*I* have a question. If the cafeteria's still open, will someone please bring me a vanilla milk shake?"

There was a friendly argument over who would do it. In the end, they all went but me. Kari and I were alone together for the first time since I'd left home.

"I think you're brave," I said, "and strong."

Kari looked puzzled. Then she smiled. "Thanks. That means a lot."

"And I'm sorry for the things I said. Before."

"It's okay, Bitte." Kari squeezed my hand.

I squeezed back. We hadn't held hands since we were little girls playing mouse games together in Minna's guest room. It felt awkward and nice.

Finally, I let go and pointed to Kari's bedside table. "What's all this?" I asked. The table was covered with gifts: a bouquet of pink rosebuds from Minna and Axel, a balloon from Jorgen, a pretty new nightgown from Mamma. There were gifts for you, too, Isabella: the elephant from Angus, knitted booties from the nurses. Even Pappa had brought a tiny package that rattled when I shook it.

I didn't have a gift for you. I wanted to give you something special, something nobody else could give you. While Kari described the other presents, an idea began to grow. An idea for the perfect gift. Or so I thought. It was the kind of gift I couldn't buy. I would have to create it myself. I didn't realize at the time how long it would take, but I was eager to share my idea with you.

"Where's the baby," I asked. I hadn't seen you in the nursery on the way in.

"She's down the hall with her parents," Kari said.

This time I didn't flinch at the word *parents*. "I like them," I said. "I see why you liked them, too. They seem . . ." I hesitated. What I wanted to say was they seemed like people who would hold on tight, Isabella, and never let you go. Instead I said, "Nice. They seem nice."

I wanted to tell Kari about my becoming a woman and how I understood certain things more than I had before, but the family came back right then.

Mamma handed Kari her milk shake. After she had sipped it all down, slowly and gratefully, I decided I couldn't wait any longer. Kari and Mamma had already held you and hugged you and heard your small voice. It was my turn.

"When can we see the baby?" I asked.

Mamma checked her watch. "Any minute now," she answered. She patted Kari's shoulder. Axel and Jorgen and Pappa moved closer to Kari's bedside. I looked at Axel. "Hello-good-bye," he murmured.

Kari bowed her head and covered her eyes with her hands. I looked away. Was Kari crying? Praying? I didn't know.

I was closest to the door, so I saw it open first. Hope peeked in and said hello. "Is now a good time?" she asked.

Kari raised her head. She smoothed her quilt and nodded. "Come in."

Hope opened the door even wider and Jacob came through with you in his arms. You, Isabella. My heart raced like Axel's big car engine.

"She's beautiful," Jacob said to Kari, "just like you."

You *were* beautiful, Isabella. Hope caught me staring. "Would you like to hold her?" she asked.

It was my chance. It was what I'd been waiting for all those months, so I don't know why I said, "No, thank you."

"Go ahead, Bitte," said Kari. "She won't break."

I have to admit, Isabella, it wasn't you I was worried about. When I reached for you, my arms trembled.

Hope lifted you from Jacob's arms and showed me how to cradle your head. I found myself holding a sweet-smelling, soft-snuggling bundle of life! Your warmth flowed to every part of me. There was so much I wanted to tell you, Isabella, so much I wanted to say, but there wasn't time. I did the next best thing. I walked you to the window. I raised your little head to the night sky.

"Look," I whispered. "Do you see it?"

You scrunched up your face and waved your tiny fists in the air. I've heard newborns can't see much, so you probably didn't see the Little Bear. But I believe you saw the big golden yellow glow. I believe you saw the moon.

I put my face close to yours. My cheek brushed

against your velvet skin. Without thinking, I began to hum. You settled into the crook of my arm. As I rocked side to side, foot to foot, our bodies seemed to melt together. You closed your eyes. Your delicate eyelashes rested on your cheeks in two peaceful curves. I hummed and rocked, rocked and hummed the lullaby my favorite aunt had sung to me. I sounded just like Minna. I sounded just like Auntie Me.

I'll tell you something, Isabella. I held on to that moment long after I carried you to my sister and gently placed you in her arms.

"Did you notice, Bitte? She has my nose." Kari touched your button nose, your little toes and fingers, your tiny ears. "Oh," she said. "Mmmmm." She hugged you to her chest.

You started to whimper.

I held my breath. In my fairy-tale dreams, you never cried, Isabella. In my fairy-tale dreams, you were never sad.

Kari's own eyes filled with tears at your whimpering.

But Jacob calmly handed her a bottle. When she put it to your mouth, your whimpering stopped.

I let out a sigh of relief.

Kari fed you for a long time, but looking back, Isabella, it went by much too quickly—you sucking noisily, the rest of us drinking you in.

Then your bottle was empty. Kari lifted you to her

shoulder to rub your back. When your little baby burp came up, we all cheered softly, as if you had recited the Gettysburg Address.

"You are so smart," Kari cooed. "I love you so much." She looked up at Jacob and Hope. "Take good care of her. Tell her I love her." She kissed your forehead.

My chest tightened, Isabella, and my pulse began to pound in my ears because Kari was saying good-bye. No, I thought. I'm not ready. Then, like a constellation coming into focus for the first time, something became clear to me: I wasn't the one who needed to be ready. So I stood by my sister, Isabella. I stood with my family on one side of Kari and faced Hope and Jacob on the other side. To anyone else it might have looked like Us and Them, on the opposite sides, with you in the middle. But it wasn't that way.

The rest I remember in slow motion.

Kari gently wrapped you in her quilt.

Hope bent down and put her arm around my sister. Mamma bent down and put *her* arm around my sister. Suddenly we were all leaning toward you, our arms reaching out and holding each other: Kari holding Mamma holding Pappa holding me holding Jorgen holding Axel holding Jacob holding Hope holding Kari holding you, Isabella, our baby.

It was then I saw it: Love. I'll never forget it. Love. We were all filled to bursting with it because of you,

Isabella. Love. It passed between us, back and forth, and around and around and around.

"What do *you* think love is?" Claire asked, when summer was over and we were back in school.

"I think it's different for everyone," I said, "but trust me, you'll know it when you see it."

"Just tell me what it looks like," Claire begged.

"It looks like a circle," I said. "Love is a circle, full as the moon."

Claire laughed. "No, really, give me a hint."

Sometimes, Isabella, the simplest things are the hardest to explain.

EPILOGUE

I call you Isabella.

When I think about you, I think about the others: Minna, Axel, Jacob, Hope, Mamma, Pappa, Jorgen, Angus, and Kari. Separate but linked together, we are all part of the same constellation.

Name it what you like.

Hope and Jacob send news of you to my sister, Kari. She memorizes the letters. She treasures the pictures. Kari knows you are in good hands. She speaks of you with tenderness.

As for me, I carry you in my heart. Every year on your birthday, I light candles and whisper your name and celebrate Love. Tonight the candles shine like the stars. Twelve stars, Isabella.

Twelve.

I wonder if you've opened my gift, the one I began

twelve years ago today. I wonder if you've read the story of your beginning and if you've discovered the answer to the question, How did I get here?

I stare at the twelve tiny flames and ask myself, Was it the perfect gift after all? Will it help her understand?

I blow out the candles and make a wish.